ABOUT THE AUTHOR

George G. Gilman was born in 1936 in what was then a small village east of London. He attended local schools until the age of fifteen. Upon leaving school he decided to become a professional writer, with strong leanings towards the mystery novel. Wrote short stories and books during evenings, lunch hours, at weekends, and on the time of various employers while he worked for an international newsagency, a film company, a weekly book-trade magazine and the Royal Air Force.

His first short (love) story was published when he was sixteen and the first (mystery) novel appeared ten years later. He has been a full-time writer since 1970, writing mostly Westerns which have been translated into a dozen languages and have sold in excess of 16 million copies. He is married and lives on the Dorset coast, which is as far west as he intends to move right now.

The EDGE series by George G. Gilman
published by New English Library:

Brutal Border

George G. Gilman

NEW ENGLISH LIBRARY

A New English Library Original Publication, 1986

First NEL Paperback Edition June 1986

NEL Books are published by
New English Library,
Mill Road, Dunton Green,
Sevenoaks, Kent.
Editorial office: 47 Bedford Square, London WC1B 3DP

Typeset by Hewer Text Composition Services, Edinburgh

Printed and bound by Hunt Barnard Printing Ltd, Aylesbury, Bucks

British Library C.I.P.
Gilman, George G.
    Brutal border.—(Edge; 52)
    Rn: Terry Harknett   I. Title   II. Series
    823'.914[F]   PR6058.A686/

ISBN 0 450 39152 3

for
C.J.
even if she does prefer
a Magnum to a colt .45

1

IT WAS just as the bartender in the saloon at Lowry had told him. When he was two hours of easy riding west of town and a lot longer than that from getting to Yuma, a spur cut off to the south. At the start of the spur was an old timber signpost, hard to read because of the bleaching effect of the sun and the way it had been scoured by wind-blown dust. The arm of the sign pointed down the spur and proclaimed it led to US Army Fort Devlin, two miles distant.

'Only it don't, Mr Edge,' the slow-talking, sad-eyed, slack-mouthed bartender qualified. 'Not no more. Not just to the fort. That spur takes you into Crooked Creek where you'll likely run across this Cutler character I spoke of. Him or somebody who'll know where to find him. See, Fort Devlin's just a part of Crooked Creek these days. Town got started after the army was through putting down most of the Apache troubles around here. Of course, some of it started up again. But ain't nothing like it used to be. Reason Jefferson Cutler is doing what he's doing. Which maybe is making the Apache trouble worse, some say. But in my opinion . . .'

Edge had left the garrulous bartender then, to go to bed in one of the squalid rooms at the rear of the malodorous saloon. Uninterested in the man's opinions or the views at second hand of his fellow citizens. It was not particularly early when he bedded down, but the half-breed had the kind of constitution which did not demand many hours of sleep out of each twenty-four. So he felt well rested when he left town the next morning just as dawn was beginning to

9

grey the skies above this expanse of south western Arizona Territory. He held the chestnut gelding to an easy walk, even though both mount and rider would have relished an invigorating canter through the early morning that was still chilled by night air. Then, halfway to where the bartender had said the spur cut off the trail, the first rays of the new day's sun spilled out of Sonora and washed gently over man and animal to cast their shadows at a grotesque length ahead and to the right. By the time Edge made the turn off the Lowry to Yuma trail the entire orb of the sun was above the distant ridges of the Sierra Madre and the intensity of its dazzling glare was matched by the fierceness of its heat. And neither the half-breed nor the gelding beneath him had the slightest desire to exert themselves in any way.

Unless, in the case of the man called Edge, there was a wad of bills to make the effort worthwhile. And, by several accounts heard out along the many trails between Pomona in Texas and Lowry, which he had reached last night, a man named Jefferson Cutler was paying big bucks for the right kind of help. From what he heard of the wealthy man's requirements, Edge figured he could be the right kind.

It was a lot of miles and many days and nights between Pomona and here, but having reached his conclusion and made the decision to head for Crooked Creek unless something more promising turned up on the way there, he gave no further thought to the matter. For it was in the future and there was nothing so unpredictable as that. Now, as he neared the end of the long ride, the impassive set of his heavily-bristled features truly showed that his mind remained unconcerned about its outcome.

When he turned off the main trail he rolled and lit his second cigarette of the day. And this lasted him until he came within sight of his destination: albeit at a distance over which his view of the community was distorted by the shimmering band of heat haze that kept the cloudless blue sky from meeting the predominantly grey land to the south. He paid no more attention to the cluster of buildings than to any other aspect of his otherwise desolate surroundings as he closed with the town that he guessed was named for the arroya alongside which the spur trail ran. For, out of a habit instilled by hard-learned lessons, the half-breed kept a wary watch for possible trouble in every direction as he rode through this stretch of the arid Yuma Desert between the eastern end of the Gila Mountains and the Mexican border.

This instinctive surveillance required little conscious effort, and the information gathered by the apparently casual glances he cast about him was automatically registered or rejected by his mind in terms of how the features of his surroundings might affect him. Thus was he aware that the spur was almost as well used as the main trail, by saddle horses and team-drawn wagons. And that the creek beside the trail was likely a dry wash for the greater part of the year. For the rest . . . There were sand ridges, rock outcrops, expanses of low brush and scattered clumps of cacti spread far into the distance to either side of the trail and creek. Just like on the floor of countless other pieces of desert terrain the half-breed had ridden: both north and south of the border.

Then he was beside the marker, newer and easier to read than the signpost, that bore the name of the community. The lettering crudely painted in black on a length of untreated lumber supported at either end by stakes with the bark still on them. Or maybe, Edge reflected fleetingly, the man who painted the town marker had purposely made the lettering spidery, in keeping with the name.

'You in any mood to listen to some advice?' a man asked sourly as the half-breed shifted his gaze after a double-take at the town marker with its appropriately malformed lettering.

'Long as it doesn't commit me to taking it.'

Just as he had ridden across country much like this before so, too, had Edge been in a whole bunch of towns pretty much like this one. And in occasional towns—not all of them like Crooked Creek—he had come across lawmen who wore the same kind of life-wearied face as the one who looked at him now.

'It's a free country. Advice I'm givin' is free. Stay down

11

this end of the street for awhile. If you don't it could maybe cost you your life.'

'Much obliged, Sheriff.'

The man shrugged away the gratitude, and responded: 'It's no skin off my nose. Either way.'

Like most frontier towns, particularly those off the main trails, Crooked Creek had just the one street. And like most communities that had sprung up in the vicinity of an army post, it was the fort that dominated the town.

Fort Devlin was at the far, western end of the street: something over a quarter of a mile away from where Edge sat his reined-in horse beside the town marker. Some way back from where the street went off the trail at a right angle, the dry-bedded Crooked Creek swung to the west. Then arced around the rear of the fort before it curved east and thence south: to once again run alongside the trail that headed toward the border. This section of the trail was less well travelled than that to the north. Both in his approach to the town and now that he was there, Edge saw the fort as little more than a brown adobe wall that was something over twenty-five feet high, and he judged each of the four walls to be about a hundred yards in length. Ever since he had ridden close enough to see clearly against the shimmering of heat, he had seen the Stars and Stripes hanging limply from a pole at the top centre of the front wall. Now he could see there were large double gates in the wall beneath the flag. And some dirty grey woodsmoke was smudging the sky above the top of the wall.

Until the lawman had spoken, the smoke from behind the blank walls of Fort Devlin provided the only sign of life in the community as the time of day approached, in the half-breed's estimation, seven o'clock. For no fires had been lit in stoves to cook breakfast or heat coffee beneath any other chimneys in town. And there were no other visible signs of current human occupation in any of the single story adobe, timber or field stone buildings that flanked the broad street between the marker and the closed gates in the wall that dwarfed them. Nor a sound until the voice ended the silence that followed the halting of the horse.

'I'm looking for Jefferson Cutler,' Edge said, and shifted the direction and focus of his gaze as a low but harsh sound reached down the street.

A short-lived sound, of one of the double gates in the wall of the fort swinging open just two or three feet. So that a half dozen uniformed men could file out. While this was happening, many more men in the blue and yellow of the United States Cavalry showed themselves at the top of the wall to either side of the flag that now began to stir listlessly: moved by a high current of hot air that came no lower. Only the heads and shoulders of the men up there could be seen, so they obviously had secure footing on a walkway.

'Figured you might be.'

Now that the army had put in an appearance the civilian population of Crooked Creek was stirred out of tense silence. People coughed, shuffled their feet, exchanged low-toned answers for questions, opened doors and raised windows: but did not show themselves in the manner of the soldiers at the fort and the sheriff of the threshold of a shack that was the first building on the south side of the street, directly across from the marker.

He had needed to duck his head to step out from the shack doorway, for he was almost a match for the half-breed's six feet two inches height. But he was maybe twenty pounds less than Edge's two hundred pounds of weight, and his build was thin instead of being lean. He was past fifty, so had a few years on the stranger to town. His skin was as deeply scored by passing time and was darkly burnished by the elements. Edge's skin tone was darker, but this had as much to do with the Mexican blood of his father as with the burning suns and biting winds of his drifting existence. The sheriff's hair was thin and grey, in stark contrast with the thick-growing black hair that Edge wore down to his shoulders—with just a strand of lighter colour here and there. The half-breed's Mexican-style moustache was barely discernible on mornings such as this when he had not taken the time to shave. The man at the doorway of the adobe shack had a lush moustache of evenly mixed brown and white that did not droop at either side of his broad, thick-lipped mouth. He had brown eyes, round and a little bulging that seemed not to have viewed any aspect of the world with enthusiasm for a very long time. There was a similar quality about the eyes of the half-breed, which were light blue and glinted coldly from between lids that hardly ever cracked open wider than they did now as he studied the man at the doorway for stretched seconds.

'No offence,' the lawman said.

The man was unafraid, Edge thought, but figured it cost him nothing to be polite in this situation with a hard man—who maybe looked like a lot of others Jefferson Cutler's offer had drawn to Crooked Creek.

'Sure,' Edge allowed as he completed his study of the tall, thin man who was dressed in a check shirt, dark pants and spurless riding boots, and held a Stetson down at his left side: and carried a Frontier Colt in a holster slung from the side of his gunbelt that was fully stocked with spare shells. His clothing and revolver, like the man, were past their prime.

Then the half-breed once more shifted his attention along the street, responding to a motion of the lawman's head and the sound of a door that was wrenched open. Saw that another door must have been opened, less noisily, for there were two men moving on the street in the bright, hot sunlight of the quiet morning. One of them angling away from the front of a frame church on the north side of the street closer to the fort than to the end from which Edge and the sheriff watched. The other stepping out of the shadow cast by an adobe building three removed from that out of which the lawman had emerged.

A rippling of subdued sounds, including many curtailed gasps, greeted the abrupt but not unexpected appearance of the men. Who continued to move catty-cornered until they were on the centre of the street: then approached each other in a straight line, inexorably reducing the one hundred and fifty feet distance that had separated them when they changed direction.

'The guy who came out of the church is Billy Burroughs,'

the sheriff said in a grim-toned whisper, funereal before anybody was dead. 'The guy with his back to us is Duke Emmet. My opinion is that somebody like you could fill both vacancies.' His tone had altered from dour to sour and he spat out of the side of his mouth, like he could taste his bitterness. Then he added: 'They're shit and I figure you're better than that.'

Maybe there was an implication that the embittered man was not sure how much better he rated the half-breed, but Edge was unconcerned by the jaundiced attitudes of the sullen-humoured sheriff. He did note something that was rasped, though: that the man with the badge pinned to the left breast pocket of his check shirt was certain both men shaping for a morning showdown were destined to die.

This as Burroughs and Emmet closed to within a hundred feet of each other, their pace resolutely unhurried, the right hand of each man not moving through such a long arc as his left: so that the slightly curved fingers were never more than six inches from a pistol butt jutting from a holster. Both revolvers were Frontier Colts. That of the twenty-five-year-old, slightly built Burroughs had a smooth wooden grip. The five years older and taller, more solidly built Emmet carried a handgun with a standard metal grip.

There was an elongated damp patch of sweat on Emmet's grey shirt, between his shoulder blades. Burroughs was blinking a great deal. Little spurts of dust rose as each boot heel was set down. Some loose change chinked in somebody's pocket. A man coughed. A horse whinnied. From inside the shack behind the sheriff, a woman began to ask:

'Hey, Sterling, why are you takin' the trouble to watch——'

'Shut up, Jessica,' he cut in on her dully, without rancour.

It was inevitable that Edge, like anyone else, should find his attention concentrated on a series of inconsequential details in such a tense situation that did not involve him. The kind of guns the men carried, the way they sweated or blinked. The dust disturbed by their slow-moving feet. Also, in such a circumstance where imminent death was certain, some people in the audience were unable to remain silent or still. The cough, the coins, the words. Maybe even the horse sensed that a life was about to end and felt the need to express equine nervousness.

Having got beyond the stage of allowing his gaze to be momentarily fixed upon unimportant components of the doom-laden tableau being staged on the centre of the street, the half-breed made no effort to block out stray notions from his mind. For right now he was in no danger, of that he was certain.

The two Stetson-hatted, darkly-garbed men who were facing up to the threat of violent death, closed to within fifty feet of each other. And now there was just the sounds of their progress on the dust-powdered, hard-packed surface of the street to keep the silence in Crooked Creek from being absolute. The ears of the chestnut gelding were rigidly pricked, and Edge's mind entertained yet another quick to come and go image—of horses behind the walls of Fort Devlin and out back of the civilian buildings responding in like manner to the atmosphere generated by the two men who had chosen to put their lives on the line.

Then, underlying the faint taint of woodsmoke that continued to rise lazily into the languid air above the fort, Edge was sure he detected a hint of the smell of frying bacon. But before this sensation, triggered out of reality or by a whim of imagination, could draw a response from his gastric juices, his glinting-eyed gaze was captured by a movement. Several yards removed from Billy Burroughs and Duke Emmet, who had noticeably reduced the never-hurried cadence of their gait as they advanced to within twenty yards of one another.

A third man had shown himself to take a role in this final act of somebody's life. Then a fourth. And Edge suddenly had complete understanding of what the ill-humoured sheriff had meant when he made mention of two vacancies.

Both Burroughs and Emmet had been hired on by Jefferson Cutler: that much had been obvious at the outset.

16

What had now become apparent was that the rich man who hired them intended that neither should survive the confrontation. For the two latecomers to the scene had their guns aimed and ready to fire—Winchesters angled down from their shoulders as they came erect on building roofs. One of them on the north side of the street, his rifle targeted on the back of Burroughs. The other with his repeater trained similarly on Emmet from the south side.

Just for part of a second Edge considered the possibility that the riflemen on the roofs were positioned there to ensure fair play at the showdown. But he had rejected this even before the cavalrymen in sight at the fort and the civilians who watched from the cover of the buildings had begun to vent sounds of shock and shouts of warning.

This as the two men on the street came to a halt within ten feet of each other. And froze at the start of turning and ducking into the gunfighter's crouch. For the first time in many stretched seconds found themselves able to unlock their gazes.

Edge could see only the face of Billy Burroughs: that seemed suddenly to be the countenance of somebody much younger as its expression altered from hatred-fired determination to fear. This as he saw the shadow of the rifleman who covered Emmet.

Without tunnel vision for the eyes of Burroughs, the bigger-framed man became abruptly aware of the portentous form on the periphery of the scene before him: to the right and high up.

'Duke!' Burroughs shrieked, terror pitching his tone almost girlishly high. And he extended the turn he had started to make, intent upon getting off a shot at the man menacing Emmet as he slid the Colt from his holster.

'Frig you, Cutler!' Emmet snarled at the top of his voice. And threw himself to the ground as he drew, screwing around through the plunge in an effor. to bring his revolver to bear on the same target as Burroughs.

The watchers had been hushed by the new twist to the drama. And there was a sliver of time between the desperate shouts of the two men and the opening shots when the silence in the hot morning was once again absolute. Then the first two reports sounded. And Duke Emmet was hit in the belly, flipped into a sprawl on his back. At the same moment as Billy Burroughs took a bullet in the centre of his back and began to stagger forward. Second shots were blasted from the Winchesters, spaced a little further apart than the first two. Emmet was hit in the crotch and screamed. Burroughs made no sound audible to the watchers as the next bullet tore into his back, left of centre, and doubtless found his heart. But a third shot was triggered down at him and by freak or skilled marksmanship smashed into the back of his skull. Then, as the blood ceased to ooze from the three wounds in the back and head of his victim, the man on the roof to the north side of the street swung his Winchester down from his shoulder to slant it across his chest in a double handed grip.

But the other rifleman was not yet finished. Seemed to be spurred into a sadistic rage by Duke Emmet's pitiful attempts to rise up off the street. A second bullet into the belly caused the doomed man to let go of his revolver so that he could clutch at the fresh wound with both hands. The next shot missed and kicked up dust and a divot of sun-baked earth. Blood blossomed out across the pants and shirt of the agonised man, spreading from under his clawed hands. He gaped his mouth wide, either to give vent to his pain or to curse the man responsible. Then his body became lax, his hands slid to the ground at either side and his facial muscles were slackened. He was dead. Still and silent. But for a few more seconds he was not allowed to rest there in peace where his life ended. For five or six more rapidly-fired shots impacted into his flesh, causing the corpse to twitch and spasm. And only then, when Duke Emmet's clothing was bullet-holed and stained with blood from the centre of his chest to mid-thigh did his killer call a halt. Ported his repeater in a slovenly series of moves that seemed to mock the uniformed men on the walkway and at the gateway of Fort Devlin.

Absolute silence came to the scene again, and endured

for many stretched seconds while the killers peered down at the bullet-riddled, crimson-drenched results of their shooting: and the witnesses to the merciless executions came to terms with their feelings about what they had seen.

The sheriff sighed and slowly shook his head, like he had just seen somebody commit a misdemeanour he had been too late to prevent. Started away from the shack doorway as he said to Edge: 'Like I said, two vacancies. Did I mention they were with Jefferson Cutler?'

'You said enough for me to figure it out for myself, Sheriff,' the half-breed answered.

'Take care, lover!' Jessica urged anxiously from within the shack.

'You ever known Sterling Schroder to put his nose in business that ain't none of his concern, honey?' the lawman growled as he headed on along the street, moving not much faster than had Burroughs and Emmet when they thought they were engaged in a personal gunfight.

As Schroder moved away from the shack, the soldiers on the ground filed back into the fort and the gate was closed. And most of those on the walkway went from sight, just four remaining to patrol the walls as sentries. Within many of the buildings that flanked the street the sounds of day to day activity began to be heard, with no tenor to them that suggested the start of the morning routine had been delayed by a double killing. And now that the final traces of the acrid scent of black powder smoke had been neutralised in the hot air, the gelding beneath Edge laid back his ears.

'Howdy?' Jessica greeted phlegmatically, drawing the half-breed's gaze away from the men on the roofs as they went from sight on the blind sides of the buildings that had been their vantage points.

She had emerged from the doorway recently vacated by the lawman. At less than five and a half feet tall she had no need to duck her head, which was hugged by short cut red hair: a colour that made her blue eyes show green. She had a pale complexion, and this emphasised the dark patches under her too-small eyes. Her mouth was full and her nose fleshy, this latter probably meaning she had never been pretty: even as a child. Now she was a woman a few years on the wrong side of forty. And perhaps on other days and in different circumstances she could take the time and make herself look better than slatternly. She looked to have a slender body that could be alluring were it not attired in dark-hued baggy pants, a shapeless blouse and a threadbare serape.

'How you doing?' Edge responded.

She grimaced and said: 'I guess you figure killings on the street of Crooked Creek ought to be the business of the local sheriff, stranger?' She had the kind of voice that suggested she was well educated in the distant past, but needed still to make an effort to disguise the fact.

The half-breed told her: 'I'm here to see Jefferson Cutler. Happy to let others get on with what they figure is their business, ma'am.'

She pulled a face that perhaps indicated her view of his philosphy, or maybe was directed at the fly that zoomed in at her and she swatted away with a finely-shaped hand.

'If decent people get killed here in town, Sterling'll take care of it. What you've just seen is somebody drop shit in the street. That's against the law here. Cutler brought the shit here and Sterling's going to make sure Cutler cleans it up. And if you've come here to hire on with Jefferson Cutler, I reckon that makes you a piece of the same stuff.' The scowl became more firmly fixed on her plain face as she concluded: 'I ain't so polite as Sterling. And you can take offence if you want to take it, stranger.'

Edge eyed her bleakly, his ice blue gaze travelling the length of her from her red head to her moccasined feet. Then he tipped his hat to her and heeled his horse forward as he growled: 'I can be as polite as the sheriff, Mrs Schroder. All I want to take from you is my leave.'

2

THE UNATTRACTIVE, shabbily garbed woman at the doorway of the adobe shack laughed harshly without humour. Then shouted after the slow-riding man, her voice loud enough for half the town to hear her: 'Decker's the name! Sterling Schroder and me ain't married, wise guy! Just damn good friends!'

Edge glanced back at her and responded evenly: 'Figure that makes the sheriff a wise guy, too. Marriage can be the fastest way to end a good friendship.'

She withdrew into the shack and forcefully closed the door. Its slam was the delayed punctuation to Jessica Decker's pronouncement: which in combination had been the loudest sounds in town since the barrage of rifle fire ended. Only Sheriff Schroder took any notice of it: after the crash of the door into the frame switched his world-weary gaze from the eastern end of the street to the west. Continued to stand on the centre of the street midway between the two bullet-riddled corpses on which flies were crawling and buzzing frantically as they fed on the fast-drying spilled blood. He was watching the two men who had made the street a killing ground. They were ambling with their rifles sloped to their shoulders toward the last building on the north side of the street.

Like many others, this had a sign on the façade to proclaim its purpose. When the half-breed had ridden close to where the lawman stood, his angle of view was wide enough to the end of the street for him to be able to read the lettering on the frame building: *Tolliver's Livery. Top service. Good rates.*

'She's not a whore,' Schroder said dully, not shifting his steady gaze from the far end of the street, even after the two riflemen had swung into the livery stable. 'These days.'

'She doesn't interest me,' Edge replied without reining in his mount.

Schroder nodded. 'I'm the only one who gives Jessica money. I support her.'

'Fine.'

Then the half-breed was too far removed from the lawman for the flat-toned, low-voiced exchange to be continued. Neither man feeling the inclination to raise his voice while one stood resolutely between the corpses and the other rode toward the timber and fieldstone building directly across the street from the livery. Which could be identified from the far side of town as the premises of a barber, with the red and white spirally striped pole angled outward from the top of the door.

The parlour was not yet open for business and so after he had dismounted and hitched his reins to the rail, Edge leaned against the rail and took out the makings. Had finished rolling a cigarette when his attention was drawn to the double doorway of Tolliver's Livery. One of the doors was swung open and the pair of riflemen emerged from the shaded interior of the building, their eyes cracked to the brightness of the morning. Edge did not think it was because they were dazzled by the sun's glare that they looked long and hard at him as he struck a match on the hitching rail and lit the cigarette. This as he studied them at reasonably close quarters for the first time. Saw they were in their mid-thirties, with elements hardened faces and powerful builds. Outfitted in much the same manner as the men they had killed—and the half-breed himself. In dark-hued, Western style clothing. The rifles were in the forward slung boots of two of the four saddles cinched to the rested-up horses they led from the livery. But both packed handguns in holsters tied down to their right thighs. Each held the reins of a pair of mounts in his left hand, leaving his right one free in close proximity to the jutting butt of a Colt .45.

'You lookin' for somethin' in particular, pal?' the one with blond hair and eyebrows called, pointedly belligerent.

'Right now I'm looking to get a shave, feller,' Edge answered evenly. And was aware that not just Schroder halfway down the street was suddenly showing keen interest in the talk that passed between himself and the two men at the livery stable entrance. The sentry who patrolled the front wall of Fort Devlin, some hundred feet beyond the end of the street, and the two soldiers on the side walls had halted, and were peering down on the scene. Gave it a greater degree of attention than the apparently empty terrain spread out around the post and the town.

'We ain't no barbers,' the man with a slight harelip came back. He was the one who was either not such an expert rifle shot or had chosen to take his time in the killing of Duke Emmet. 'Old man Dawkins beds down in a back room of the parlour. We don't like bein' looked at the way you're lookin' at us, pal!'

Edge gave an almost imperceptible nod, drew against his fresh cigarette and told them without rancour: 'So why don't you get the hell out of my sight?'

The man with the harelip caught his breath, deeply shocked by the challenge. His blond-haired companion groaned:

'Oh, pal. You've just——'

'With a rifle I don't claim to be better than average,' Edge broke in. This as he came rigidly upright from leaning against the rail. 'With a handgun . . .' He allowed what could have been a boast to hang unfinished in the tobacco smoke that he expelled. Paused only for a moment before he added the warning: 'But anybody points any kind of gun at me, he'd better kill me right off. Because that's what I'll do to him. First chance I get.'

'Do we look impressed, pal?' the man with the slight facial deformity challenged, his attitude contemptuous now he had recovered from unfamiliar shock.

'You don't look to be ready to shoot off more than your mouth, feller.'

'Wade! Rankinn! You get down here and haul away your

23

dirty work!' It was Schroder who ended the stretched seconds of nerve-tingling tension that came in the wake of the half-breed's even-toned counter challenge. The lawman sounded grouchily impatient rather than anxious: either unaware of the explosive situation at the end of the street or unconcerned by it.

'Wade?' the harelipped man rasped, eager to draw against Edge if his companion was ready to back the play.

'Let it go, old buddy,' he was told. 'Best we check with the major.'

He shifted his gaze from the half-breed to Rankinn, the aggression draining out of his eyes and leaving them empty of all feeling. And after Rankinn had started to move sullenly away, Wade looked again at Edge and his eyes were still like inanimate brown pebbles sunk in surrounds of white marble. And he spoke softly as he set off in the tracks of Rankinn and the other two horses, the words sounding harder than the look in his eyes:

'Maybe another time, pal. Right now you should know Fred Dawkins won't give you a shave anywhere near as close as the one you've just had.'

Edge answered: 'Just so long as he doesn't have a shaky hand, feller.'

And for part of a second the half-breed tensed again to go for his gun. This as the broad back of the blond-haired man became rigid in reaction to the barbed response. But then Wade's attitude matched that of Rankinn as the two of them led the horses toward where Schroder waited: the both of them smarting at the need to back off. And Edge guessed their resentment was made harder to bear when the trooper on the walkway above the fort gates gave vent to a gust of laughter. But this was curtailed at its peak when a commanding voice within the post snarled:

'Sentry! Can that!'

Then at the sound of a bolt being slid, Edge turned toward the barber shop. The door swung inward and a slightly-built, totally bald man of close to seventy said in ominous tones:

'Mister, you've just made two bad enemies.'

24

'I've never known any that were good,' the half-breed replied as he glanced along the street to where Wade and Rankinn were slumping the corpses over the saddles on two of the horses.

The barber did a double-take at his first customer of the day, his myopic eyes seeing the stranger to Crooked Creek close up now. And the expression on the old-timer's crinkled, leather-textured features signalled the changing of his opinion before he voiced it. 'Or maybe it's those two cold-blooded murderers who oughta beware, uh?'

Edge grinned at him and said as he advanced on the doorway and Dawkins backed inside: 'They can be wherever the hell they like, feller. Just so long as they ain't aiming guns at me. I can't abide that.'

The aroma of brewing coffee was the strongest fragrance in the barber shop. And it was only as he detected this that the half-breed became aware of the much stronger smell of woodsmoke and cooking food that scented the morning air. Now it was not just the chimneys of the Fort Devlin kitchen that expelled smoke. Cooking fires had been lit in many of the buildings of Crooked Creek. He saw this as he held back from entering the doorway to direct another glance to his left, his attention captured by the clopping of hooves.

The limp and lifeless forms of the gunshot men were being tied to their saddles, bellies down with hands and feet dangling. Schroder was moving away in the direction of a frame-built shack on the north side of the street across an alley from the church. The sheriff glanced toward the rider who had just entered town from the south trail, spat out of the side of his mouth and went from sight into the alley without breaking stride. Wade and Rankinn paused briefly in what they were doing when they saw the rider. Then made haste to complete the chore.

Fred Dawkins said: 'I certainly won't cause you no trouble in that way, sir. You can rest assured of that.'

'Uh?' Edge grunted absently as he returned his impassive gaze to the barber, having guessed from the reactions of the lawman and the two men taking care of the corpses that the newcomer was quite probably Jefferson Cutler.

The old-timer dry-washed his hands. Not afraid of the half-breed. Simply ridding himself of the final dregs of the tension he had experienced a minute or so ago. Explained, 'Was sayin' you got no worry about me pointin' any gun at you, sir. I ain't never been known to hurt no livin' thing of a purpose. Why, I can't even recall the last time I nicked a man while I was shavin' him.'

The white-jacketed Dawkins had gone to stand beside one of the two chairs in the small, cramped parlour. Now gestured for Edge to take a seat.

'Accidents I overlook,' the half-breed said as he entered. And took a final drag against the cigarette before he pinched out its fire and put it in a shirt pocket. He hooked his hat on one of a row of pegs just inside the entrance and did not shut the door behind him, then sat where he was invited and instructed: 'Just a shave.'

'Be a pleasure, sir,' the barber said brightly, and began to strope a straight razor that was far more ornate than the one Edge carried in a pouch held to the nape of his neck by a circlet of dull-coloured beads.

'That's what I'm hoping, feller.'

The old-timer's now smiling eyes met the glinting ones of his customer in the cracked and mottled mirror above a shelf on which a row of named shaving mugs were aligned. And because he was so short sighted, Fred Dawkins failed to recognise the tacit message he was being given. And he said cheerfully: 'Rest assured it will be, sir. I ain't no spring chicken in the prime of my life and I don't see so good as I used to. But I ain't makin' no idle boast when I tell you this. If I wasn't the only barber hereabouts . . . If there was a dozen more men in my line of work in Crooked Creek, I'd be the best of the bunch. It's the experience that counts more than——'

'If there were a dozen barbers in town,' Edge broke in with low-voiced insistence as the old-timer draped a towel across his chest and shoulders, 'I'd give my business to the one who talked the least.'

The crinkled face lost its animated expression and Dawkins said earnestly: 'All right. You ain't like most of my customers who like me to jabber when they're bein' shaved. It's your first time with me, though. I had to sound you out. But whatever you say, sir.'

Edge closed his eyes as the comfortably padded chair was cranked to tilt him backwards. And murmured: 'Right now I like the sound of nothing.'

3

IT WOULD have been easy to drift into a shallow level of sleep as he lay back in the chair, listening to the unobtrusive noises that Fred Dawkins made. His footfalls, his faintly wheezy breathing, the pouring of hot water from a kettle into a mug and the beating up of a lather with a brush. While from outside there drifted in through the open doorway a series of muted sounds that were equally as soporific. Probably if he had been inclined to try, Edge would have been able to separate and identify the sources of the various sounds that all contributed to a general murmuring buzz of the town of Crooked Creek and the army post of Fort Devlin facing up to the start of a new day. Maybe a little later than usual.

But he did not elect to involve himself in a mental exercise of this nature to keep dangerous drowsiness at bay. Instead he hunted in his memory for the last occasion when he had set out purposefully to seek a job of work that would pay him money to feed himself and his horse. A thousand images came and went across the forefront of his mind: during the moments when the barber was preparing to shave him and then when the lather was being applied and the bristles were being smoothly scraped off with expert gentleness. But he was not able to dredge up the recollection he sought. Perhaps because it was too far back in the past. Or maybe there never had been such a time when the means to raise the wherewithal to keep body, soul and horse together had not presented itself to him when there was need? Or, more likely, he was not prepared to devote enough concentration to such a thought process.

Not while he felt the need to remain alert to the possibility that Wade and Rankinn could decide—maybe on instructions from Cutler—to complete their unfinished business with him while they were still in a killing frame of mind.

Thus did he attempt to isolate only particular sounds from the background of those made by Dawkins in the barber shop and the army and civilian inhabitants of the town beyond the open doorway: sounds that his instinct for danger would warn him were hostile.

'Can I ask you a question, sir?' Dawkins said at length. 'So I can be sure I'm doin' what you want?'

A man's footfalls had approached the barber shop and come to a halt just beyond the threshold. Edge was conscious of being studied by eyes other than those of the old-timer as he replied:

'No sweat.'

'You seem to be startin' a moustache, sir. Unless your beard grows more strongly where it seems to——'

'Leave it, feller. It's not new. I keep it trimmed back.' He raised his voice slightly to address the man at the doorway. 'I'm nearly through. The shave is all I'm having.'

'But not, I think, what you came to Crooked Creek to get?' the newcomer said, his voice smoothed by a cultured background spent mainly in the south.

'Mornin' to you, Major Cutler, sir,' the white-jacketed old-timer greeted with a brand of politeness that stopped just short of being obsequious.

'Dawkins,' the man paying big bucks for the right kind of help countered dismissively. This as he stepped through the doorway and then continued to address Edge. 'I'm given to understand by the sheriff here that you came to this area to see me?'

'That's it, all through,' the barber announced, cheerful again now that his customer's dictate for silence had been rescinded. He cranked the chair into its upright position as he raised the towel for Edge to mop at the left-over lather on his face and neck. 'Be ten cents if you're happy with what I did for you, sir.'

The half-breed briefly surveyed his freshly shaved face in

the ancient and discoloured mirror. Then nodded as he handed the towel to Dawkins and told the man: 'You're right, feller. You are good at your trade.'

'Just as you claim to be skilled in your line of business, I'm given to understand?' Jefferson Cutler said as Edge came out of the chair with a certain reluctance, flexing the muscles of his arms and shoulders after the comfortable respite. 'By Mr Wade and Mr Rankinn.'

The half-breed gave Fred Dawkins a dime and took the partially smoked cigarette from his shirt pocket. Angled it from a side of his mouth before he looked at the man he had ridden so many miles to see. And said as he struck a match on the butt of his holstered revolver: 'My line of business isn't shooting people, Mr Cutler.' He lit the cigarette.

'It's Major Cutler, mister. Then it would seem we have nothing to discuss. Since right now I'm only looking for people prepared to kill other people.'

Edge went to get his hat from the peg near the doorway as he replied: 'I sometimes need to kill people in whatever happens to be my line of business.'

'That's a rather fine distinction, Mr . . ?'

'Edge. I've always made it.'

Cutler had the bearing of a military man and looked as elegant and well-bred as he sounded. He was in his mid-fifties or perhaps he was a well preserved sixty. Close to six feet tall, he had a well-built frame which was just starting to run to fat at the waist and neck. Above his thickening neck he had a face that was now distinguished: and had probably turned a great many feminine heads when he was young. For he had once been ruggedly hand-some, his features hewn to a pattern not too angular nor classically regular. Grey hair that was thinning on top but grew bushily in long sideburns detracted a little from his good looks these latter days. Even more so did his eyes, that were closer to yellow than to brown. But it was not their colour so much as their stony lifelessness that robbed his face of its rightful attractiveness. He had a smooth skin, lightly browned by recent exposure to the sun. So he was not normally an outside soldier.

Below the neck he was dressed in the pants and vest of an expensive, high quality three-piece suit, grey in colour, a starched white shirt with a large knotted grey necktie and high polished grey shoes. He carried a glossy black cane with an ornate silver handle. He must have dusted himself off since riding into Crooked Creek, for there was just a fine coating of white on his shoes and the lower third of the cane from his walk to the barber shop.

He asked: 'May I enquire where you heard of my plans, Mr Edge?'

'A small town in Texas named Pomona.' Cutler looked surprised at this, until the half-breed added: 'From a hardware drummer on his way from El Paso to San Angelo. He was in Yuma City before El Paso. Had to pass through this area on his swing to the east.'

'I see, Mr Edge. And you travelled several hundreds of miles on the strength of what this salesman of pots and pans told you?'

The half-breed stepped out over the threshold, liking the smell of coffee too much. Cutler came out in his wake as he said: 'The drummer didn't know too many details, Major. Something about Apache trouble that the army was dragging its feet on. A man named Jefferson Cutler who was paying top dollar for men to help him take care of the Apache trouble.'

At the far end of the street, Wade and Rankinn rode their horses on to the trail south, each of them with a lead line on a second horse burdened by an unshrouded corpse. And now that just blood in the dust showed where the double killing had taken place, the citizens of Crooked Creek felt able to leave their homes and open up their business premises.

'That is an excellent encapsulation of the situation, Mr Edge,' Cutler responded as the half-breed saw that the double entrance doors of the Crooked Creek Eating House now stood open. 'Do you have a particular aversion to the Apaches yourself?'

'No.'

He was surprised again. 'But to ride so far?'

31

'I don't have too many aversions, Major. The main one, I guess, is to having guns aimed at me. But that's run pretty close by staying in a place too long. Town or country. Unless there's good reason to stick around anyplace, I drift on.'

He broke off as a shouted command caused both the gates of Fort Devlin to be swung open. Then the same voice ordered:

'Forward at a walk, walk!'

And a fourteen-strong patrol of cavalrymen rode out of the post, headed up by a youthful-looking lieutenant. The junior officer, a sergeant, two corporals and ten troopers were all smartly turned out and their mounts looked to be in good shape. Only the neatly moustached lieutenant looked anywhere but straight ahead as the patrol started along the street and the gates in the front wall of the fort clattered shut. The officer turned his head to direct a sneeringly hostile glower at Cutler.

Edge sensed that he was intended to accept a share of the uniformed man's malevolence, by association.

Cutler growled: 'Shavetail punk,' and was a little late in spreading a cold grin over his face to try to mask that he had been touched on the raw.

Along the street, which was getting busier by the moment, a wagon that had been driven in off the south trail was rolled to a halt. One of the troopers called out something to the driver of the wagon. The driver responded with a one-fingered gesture and the trooper was bawled out by the lieutenant.

The half-breed continued: 'Sometimes I don't have any particular end in mind when I drift. This time I was headed for Crooked Creek. But if something more definite had come up on the way here——'

'You have the strangest way of approaching me for employment, Mr Edge!' Cutler interrupted, his tone brittle while he still needed to salve the raw nerve exposed by the junior officer. 'Firstly you attempted to start a fight with two of my ablest men. Now your attitude suggests you are indifferent to what I have to offer.'

Edge dropped his cigarette and ground it into the dust under a heel. Said as he did this: 'Major, mostly my line of work is ending fights started by other people. I'm good at it and if you're really paying big bucks for men to help you end your fight with the Apaches, I'd like to work for you. But if my face doesn't fit, I'll just drift on out of Crooked Creek. Something will turn up, I guess. If you want to take this any further, I'll be over at the eating house for awhile. Smell of Dawkins' coffee has set my belly juices running.'

He moved to the rail and unhitched the gelding's reins. And Cutler snapped:

'It's not your face that fails to fit! It's your manner, Mr Edge! I am in the process of raising an army. A fighting force of the highest standing. And to achieve this I demand strict adherence to discipline by the men I enlist!' A frosty smile of quiet satisfaction suddenly spread across his face as he lowered his voice. 'I'm given to understand that you witnessed the execution of two of my men who broke that discipline?'

The half-breed offered no response to the rhetorical question. But when he had swung astride his mount, he told the finely dressed, rigidly erect man on the ground: 'I was a cavalry captain once. I have a lot of respect for discipline when there's need of it.'

Jefferson Cutler looked up at Edge, long and hard: dead eyes giving nothing away. Then he announced: 'I insist upon being called major, Mr Edge?'

'No sweat.'

'I pay ten dollars a day.'

'That sounds fine, Major.'

A nod. 'I have a final appointment with the commanding officer of Fort Devlin, Mr Edge. Forget that disgusting restaurant across the street. My men eat better than that. The wagon you can see is being loaded with supplies by Ben Breslin. My most trusted man. Report to him. I do not envisage being at the fort more than a few minutes. But should it take much longer, Breslin and yourself will leave for our headquarters. Sooner than he expected, since he'll have help in loading the supplies?'

Cutler had used his cane to point to the army post when he mentioned it. Then to the parked wagon, the driver of which had been involved in an ill-humoured exchange with one of the troopers a few minutes ago.

'Sure, Major,' Edge replied to the implied query, and tugged on the reins to back his horse away from the rail and turn him.

'One point that should be cleared up before we proceed, Mr Edge.' Cutler put it after a pause for thought.

Edge checked his mount and eyed the man expectantly.

'I am no longer a regular commissioned officer.'

'What I figured, Major.'

'I resigned the army at the conclusion of the War Between the States.'

'Sure, Major.'

'As a former serving officer yourself, you should perhaps be made aware that my own service was in the cause of the Confederacy.'

'I'm aware, Major.'

'You were engaged in that conflict, Mr Edge? You seem to be of an age that makes that likely?'

'I backed the winning side, Major.'

Cutler's mouth twitched and his knuckles whitened as he took a firmer grip on the silver handle of the cane. Then he murmured: 'I see.'

'No sweat, far as I'm concerned,' the half-breed told him. 'The war's been over a lot of years. Seems to me that who fought on which side is a minor matter. Major.'

'I share your opinion, Mr Edge.'

'And at your rates of pay, I'm real glad I'm no longer with the Union.'

4

BEN BRESLIN was red headed and red faced. Of Irish extraction. His round face and the way his features were set into the basic structure made him look Irish at first glance and his voice sounded like he had only just got off the boat from Cork.

'You'll have just enlisted in the major's fightin' force,' he greeted without giving away what he thought of this, as Edge reined in his gelding and swung out of the saddle at the rear of the part-loaded flatbed wagon.

'You don't read minds and nobody hears that good,' Edge replied, his own attitude equally as neutral. And glanced back up the street to where Jefferson Cutler was being admitted to Fort Devlin after an ill-humoured exchange with a sentry.

'I can see that far, friend,' Breslin countered. 'I saw you and him chewin' the fat and the major ain't no gossip. And you sure look the kind of man the major is in the market to take on. You're to ride down to San Juan with me, did he say?'

'If that's the headquarters.'

'That it is,' Breslin confirmed and turned to swing a heavy sack off his shoulder and on to the rear of the wagon. Then asked: 'Did the major say anythin' about you givin' me a hand with the supplies, friend?'

'Sure. And he metioned some good eating to be had at his headquarters. I guess the quicker the wagon's loaded, the faster we get to the chow.'

Now Breslin cracked his face with a broad smile that showed more gum than teeth and made his small eyes glint

35

with genuine humour. 'Seein' as how I'm the cook at San Juan, that sure as shootin' is the truth. And although too many cooks might spoil the broth, many hands make light work. Now isn't that the truth, friend?'

Edge hitched the gelding's reins to a rear wheel of the flatbed and joined Breslin in the chore of hauling sacks and cartons and crates from out of the grocery and the dry goods stores that were adjacent neighbours. The two of them taking the supplies from stacks that had obviously been set aside to fulfil an advance order.

Breslin said little to the half-breed or the two store-keepers as he and his new helper loaded the wagon. But he was seldom silent. Either sang or hummed snatches of romantic-sounding ballads that mostly seemed to be concerned with sparkling-eyed colleens, misty mountains, placid lakes or rolling green hills far across the sea. But although he was almost a caricature of an Irishman, Edge guessed the man had been on this side of the Atlantic Ocean for many years. Thought that probably the battered kepi in confederate colours that sat upon his shock of red hair, and the yellow sergeant's chevrons neatly sewn to the right sleeve of his civilian shirt, had been part of his own uniform when he fought for the Rebels.

He was about fifty, and overweight; perhaps from too much sampling of the food he cooked. He stood no taller than five and a half feet but probably weighed close to a hundred and eighty pounds. Not much of this was flabby fat, though, and this was mostly around his middle where his belly draped over his belt buckle. But his arms and legs, chest and back bulged with hard-looking muscles against the constraints of his dark-hued shirt and pants as he did far more than his fair share of hefting and toting the supplies from out of the stores and on to the wagon.

When the loading was complete Cutler was still inside Fort Devlin and Breslin wasted no time after a glance toward the firmly closed double gates. He climbed up on to the seat and had the brake lever forward and the reins of the two-horse team in his hands before Edge had unhitched the gelding from the rear wheel. Then asked with indifference:

'You want to ride your horse or with me, friend?'

'A saddle gives a softer ride than a wagon seat,' the half-breed answered, and stepped back quickly when the wagon was set into motion the instant he had freed his reins from the wheel.

Breslin steered the rig into a tight turn between the grocery and dry goods stores and the church that was directly across the street. After Edge had swung up into his saddle, he paused before heeling the gelding in the wake of the wagon, conscious of being studied. And saw it was Sterling Schroder who was watching him: the tall and skinny lawman standing in an open doorway that gave on to the alley beside the church. Above the doorway was a crudely painted sign that proclaimed the sheriff was on the threshold of his office. The expression on the dark, deeply-lined face beneath the thinning grey hair projected mild contempt. Then the man spat dismissively from the side of his mouth before he backed into the shack and thudded the door into the frame.

Edge followed the wagon at an easy pace, rolling a cigarette. He was not aware of attracting anything more than indifferent passing interest as he completed the ride to the end of the street, where he lit the cigarette as he swung on to the south trail. And within a few yards had overhauled the wagon.

Ben Breslin had just gotten a large-bowled pipe to draw smoothly, and he did not remove the stem from between his tightly clamped gums to say: 'I'm thinkin' hard livin' ain't nothin' new to you, friend?'

'Uh?' Edge grunted.

'Ain't nothin' wrong with a man choosin' to ride soft instead of hard when he can do either. But you look to have had most of life hard is what I'm sayin' to you?'

'Guess so, feller.'

'Then you won't mind so much that there ain't so much that's soft and easy out at San Juan. But I'm thinkin' it'll come as a shock to the system of a man like you to jump when somebody tells you to jump?'

Edge removed the cigarette, pursed his lips and replied:

37

'The major's paying big money, feller. He warned me that part of what he wanted in return was a respect for discipline. I guess we reached an understanding about that.'

He angled the cigarette from the side of his mouth again, as Breslin looked pointedly unimpressed before he matched the half-breed's impassiveness. Then he asked:

'I'm thinkin' you saw the gunplay this mornin'? Did the major say anythin' about it?'

'Said two men were executed for breaking discipline, feller.'

'He didn't tell you that I should be addressed as sergeant, friend?' He slightly raised his right arm to emphasise the chevrons sewn on the sleeve.

'Just that he should be addressed as major,' the half-breed said evenly. 'But I'm easy, Sergeant. You can call me Edge, in case it turns out I'm no friend to you.'

Breslin grinned broadly, then removed the pipe so that he could vent a gust of the kind of laughter that rocked his drooping belly. 'Friendship isn't somethin' there's much of at San Juan, Edge. But I sure as shootin' like your style. Yes, indeed.' He clamped his gums to the pipe stem again, and chuckled through what remained of his good humour.

Then Edge prompted: 'Why did Wade and Rankinn gun down Burroughs and Emmet, Sergeant?'

Enjoyment was momentarily displaced by grimness, before the round, red face became neutral. And Breslin's tone of voice was in keeping with his facial expression as he supplied: 'We've all hired on to fight a bunch of Apaches. Not each other. Word reached headquarters last night that those two meatheads had fallen out over a card game. Emmet accused Burroughs of cheatin'. And they fixed it to settle the matter on the street in Crooked Creek this mornin'. The major ordered Ray Wade and Ethan Rankinn to go to town and settle it for them, once and for all. I heard those two blackhearted sonsofbitches made quite a show of it?'

'You heard right, Sergeant. Quite a show for everybody. Including the army at the fort and the sheriff at his lady friend's house.'

Breslin nodded shortly. Gathered in some sweet-smelling smoke and allowed it to trickle out through his nostrils, like he was loath to let the fragrance get away. 'I'm thinkin' you don't know too much about the job you've hired on to do, Edge?'

'To fight Apaches for ten dollars a day about sums up what I know,' the half-breed replied.

'As part of a private army.'

'Yeah, that too. Although maybe something could come out of what the major spoke of as a final appointment with the commanding officer at Fort Devlin?'

Breslin scowled and rasped: 'Can pigs fly, friend?' Shook his head and moderated his tone and expression. 'No. Major Cutler is callin' on Colonel Crispin out of courtesy, nothin' more. The major's not the kind of officer who expects the men to respect regulations that he ignores.'

'Whatever you say, Sergeant,' Edge allowed, and drew a sharply suspicious look from the man's small eyes.

But Breslin checked the impulse to anger, unsure how to judge the half-breed's response. Confined himself to the comment: I've got good reasons for how I feel about Jefferson Cutler, friend.'

Edge countered as evenly as before: 'I've got no good reason for needing to know right now just why he's so eager to go Apache hunting.'

The man driving the wagon vented an abrupt, inarticulate sound of ill-temper. From the way in which he pointedly avoided glancing at the rider alongside the rig, Edge knew Breslin was irritated only with himself: and to use up time while he regained his composure, the red-headed man pretended his pipe had gone out and struck two unnecessary matches in the charade of re-lighting it. Eventually said, a little sheepishly:

'I'm thinkin' I'm doin' a lot of round-about talkin' without gettin' to the point, friend? Which ain't usually my way. But Billy Burroughs . . . he was one of the few men at San Juan that I liked. So I'm thinkin' it hit me harder than I'd like to admit. Him bein' punished so hard as he was.

39

Know it was right he should pay for breakin' the rules he knew about, but——'

'You've already made your point on that, Sergeant,' Edge interrupted. And again his tone offered no clue to what was in his mind when he spoke.

Breslin shot an enquiring glance at him and saw that the lean, freshly shaved, sweat-beaded face was as uncommunicative as the voice. This as the half-breed kept up the apparently casual surveillance of his surroundings that had in part pre-occupied him since he overhauled the wagon. What the hooded, narrowed glinting slits of his eyes saw were familiar enough sights to Ben Breslin. An arid desert landscape across which the trail ran in an arrow-straight line beside the gently meandering dry wash, between Crooked Creek at their backs and the humps of some low hills ahead. The town and the higher ground were both cloaked in heat haze, shimmering like the currents of air above a fire. At their sides the horizons to the east and the west were also shrouded in mirage-featured haze. Stunted brush and many varieties of the cactus with, here and there a small outcrop of rock, were all that broke up the monotonous flatness of the parched land spread to the east, the south and the west. To the north, a lone horseman was moving on the trail. Not making any strenuous efforts to catch up with the wagon and its outrider.

'Be the major, I'm thinkin', Mr Edge,' Breslin growled after double-checking the distant horseman.

'No argument, feller.'

For stretched seconds that perhaps lengthened into two minutes, there was no talk between the two men. During this period Edge took a drink from a canteen and Breslin's pipe did go out. He emptied the dottle by banging the bowl on the side of the wagon seat and then broke his silence to explain:

'When the war was over, the major and me, we went our different ways. Me, I headed for New York City and joined the police force. Nothin' fancy. Just a plain constable. The major, he came back out west with his wife and two daughters. To take up again in the horse raisin' business.

40

A place north of here called Kingstown. You heard of it? I never did. Not much of a place anyway. Not much more than the Cutler ranch and a stage line way station for the Butterfield Company. The major, he had a whole pile of money left him by his rich parents and after he used some of it to set up in the business, he made a whole lot more. By all accounts.'

He began to suck on the empty pipe, seeming to get some degree of satisfaction from the mere fact of having the stem clamped between his near toothless gums. Then went on: 'I didn't know nothin' of this back when it was all goin' fine for the major. First I knew of him since the war ended was when I read it in a New York newspaper that the Apaches had hit his place. Burned it down, killed his children and stole his wife along with a whole string of his bloodstock horses.'

He shook his head, morosely pensive. 'I'm thinkin' that maybe the newspaper would have run the account just because of the major bein' such a wealthy man. But what made it a big thing was that the major wasn't satisfied with what the army and the law was doin' to chase down the Indians and to get back Mrs Cutler. So the major, he made it known he was raisin' a fightin' force to do the job himself. And his offer of high pay was bringin' a lot of fightin' men to Crooked Creek. That's what made it so interestin' for the newspaper, I'm thinkin.'

Back on the trail to the north, the huddle of buildings that were Crooked Creek and Fort Devlin had disappeared into the heat haze. The rider, who was most certainly the man Ben Breslin was talking about, had closed to within a half mile of the trundling wagon. To the south, the rising ground was clearer to see, and in the sky above one smooth hill crest it was possible to discern dark wood smoke merged with the shimmer.

'How long ago was this?' Edge asked, and drank some more stale, too-warm water then mopped sweat off his face with a shirt sleeve.

'Somethin' over a couple of months,' Breslin answered, disinterested. Eager to get his account told without being sidetracked. 'I liked workin' in the police force in New York City, Mr Edge. But soon as I read that in the newspaper about the major, I walked out of my job and came out to Crooked Creek just as fast as I could. Train, stage and then horseback. And the chance of earnin' big money didn't have nothin' to do with me doin' that, I can tell you. Major Jefferson Cutler, he kept me from gettin' busted down from sergeant more times than I can recall when I served with him. On account of the drinkin' I used to do. More important than that, though, he twice saved me from bein' killed. At Manassas Junction right at the start. Then in the Peach Orchard on the second day at Gettysburg. Were you in the war, Mr Edge?'

'On the other side, Sergeant,' Edge answered evenly, then added without haste when the man wearing the Rebel kepi scowled: 'The major knows about it and we're of the same mind about letting the past rest where it is.'

'Could have been you tryin' to shoot our heads off at both those places I mentioned, I'm thinkin'?'

'We called Manassas Junction First Bull Run. I was there. And at Gettysburg.' He spat to the side of the trail, away from where the man on the wagon seat continued to project his bad feeling with a scowl. Then drawled: 'I guess it seemed like a good idea at the time for a lot of us to be doing what we were doing. Right now, fighting Apaches for more in a day than I was getting in a week to shoot at you Johnnie Rebs is a whole better idea, seems to me.'

'Right, friend,' Breslin agreed with an emphatic nod. 'The past is dead and gone. We're both on the same side now. But like I've told you, I'm still fightin' for a Cause. The money ain't that important to me.'

'No sweat, Sergeant.'

'You was an officer, I'm thinkin', Mr Edge? At the pay you made mention of.'

'Lieutenant at the start. Captain when I mustered out.'

'I don't know if what a man used to be in the army makes any difference at San Juan,' Breslin murmured thoughtfully, genuinely concerned about this question that had seemingly not occurred to him before.

'Except to one major and a sergeant?' the half-breed reminded.

'Hey, that's right, friend.' This time he was genuinely surprised that he had to acknowledge the fact. Then he shrugged. 'Far as I know, nobody minds about that.'

'Put me along the nobodies, sergeant,' Edge said evenly.

This drew another double-take from Breslin, whose account of being on the New York City police force acted to stress still further his Irishness. Then the half-breed's sardonic expression triggered a burst of belly shaking laughter from the man on the wagon, who slapped a thigh with an open palm and exclaimed: 'Glory be, do I like your style, Mr Edge. Ain't many men of your kind who can laugh at themselves. You've got some of Old Ireland in you someplace, I'm thinkin'?'

'Mexican and Scandinavian is as far back as I can go, Sergeant.'

'You don't say?'

'Ma was a Swede and they aren't supposed to have much of a sense of humour. But I figure she must have had, to marry my Pa.'

The light-hearted exchange based on inconsequentials had allowed time for Jefferson Cutler to close with the wagon so that the clop of his mount's hooves could be heard in competition with those of the team horses and the half-breed's gelding. When the red faced, red headed man became aware of this, he curtailed his enjoyment of the talk. And said, his voice lowered to a whisper before there was need:

'The major used to have a real keen sense of humour himself, Mr Edge. But I'm thinkin' the Apaches killed that part of what he is.'

This instituted another silence between Breslin and Edge. And the next words to be spoken were addressed to Cutler. By the long ago non-com to the man who was his contempory major:

'All the supplies as ordered are aboard, sir. Mr Edge informed me you ordered him to report to me for duty.'

'Supplied and paid for, Ben,' the man with dead eyes in

43

a distinguished face responded in a less than military manner. Then seemed to disprove what Breslin had announced about his lack of a sense of humour when he added: 'The goods you got from the stores in Crooked Creek I mean. Not our new recruit.'

But there was no lightness in his tone and not the trace of even a cold smile on his features. Edge shot a glance at the man as he slowed his horse to match the pace of the team on the other side of the rig. And saw that Cutler was pre-occupied with a line of thought that troubled him. At the same time that the half-breed discerned this, Breslin directed a warning frown at him, tacitly suggesting it would be better to let the major open a conversation—if that was the way the major wanted it.

But Edge ignored this to ask: 'You didn't get what you wanted out of the commanding officer at Devlin, Major?'

Breslin cleared his throat: an archetypal non-com poised to bawl out an enlisted soldier for daring to by-pass the chain of command to an officer. But Cutler spoke first.

'Has Ben told you anything of what I have it in mind to do, Mr Edge?' he asked without turning his head. Continued to peer directly along the trail that was now running beside the dry wash on a curving line through the fold between two hills.

'About your two daughters being killed and your wife kidnapped, Major. We were just getting to why the army and the law gave up the chase.'

'I didn't go into no details, sir,' Breslin was quick to explain, still concerned about how Cutler might react to future questions which could be in the mind of the half-breed.

'In a word, Mr Edge, diplomacy,' Cutler said dully, ignoring the man on the wagon. And maintaining his unwavering gaze on the way ahead: but in a manner that suggested he was not seeing the dusty trail, pebble-bedded arroyo or the barren slopes of the flanking hills. 'Not so very far south of this point is the border with Mexico. It was at Kingstown, some twenty miles to the north, that the band of renegade Indians wrote the end to my life as I had known it. Burned my home and everything in it. Stole some of the finest bloodstock stallions and mares outside of Europe. Stripped my two young daughters naked: they were seven and ten. And strung them from tree branches by their ankles and lit fires beneath their heads. Presumably while my wife was forced to witness such barbarism. Then took my wife with them.'

'Major!' Breslin attempted to check the man who was telling of the atrocity in a monotoned voice. This after he had directed a censuring scowl at the half-breed riding on the other side of the wagon.

'It's all right, Ben,' Cutler assured. Still seemingly detached from everything about his surroundings except his two companions. Then he cleared his throat and his face expressed a fleeting frown, as if he had to think deeply to pick up the threads of what he was saying and the memory lapse irritated him. At length he went on: 'I was in San Antonio looking at new stock when it happened. There had been no hint of any trouble from hostile Indians before I left. But trouble there was.

'I told it selfishly. Four hands were shot down as they attempted to defend my family and property. A Butterfield stage coach was held up, robbed and the passengers massacred. Some homesteads were attacked and the men, women and children on them were murdered. The death toll was twenty-three during the day and a night of the slaughter, Mr Edge.

'I suppose the military and civil authorities did what they could in the immediate aftermath of the attacks. But the band of Apaches who went on the rampage bolted for Mexico when their blood lust was satisfied. And the chase was halted at the border.

'Since then, the governments of our country and Mexico have been involved in negotiations that may soon allow the United States army and Federal lawmen to cross the border. For the purpose of apprehending the Apache renegades. Perhaps the Federales will co-operate in rounding up the Indian savages. But these negotiations are being conducted at the highest level, Mr Edge. And Washington and Mexico City are a great distance apart. No agreement

45

has yet been reached, I'm given to understand. Or if it has word has not been communicated to local level—to Colonel Crispin at Fort Devlin.'

His expression had grown grim and his tone had become embittered as he spoke of dilatory diplomacy. Breslin was obviously about to interrupt again, but Cutler did not allow a long enough pause.

'From the outset, I did not expect fast action, Mr Edge,' he went on. And now his expression and tone were of determination to the total exclusion of emotion. 'I commenced to raise my private army at once. And was warned then that I and my men faced serious repercussions if we took the law into our own hands to cross the border and hunt down the Apaches.

'This morning I went for the final time to Fort Devlin. To hear if any communication had been received from Washington. It had not. And Colonel Crispin felt duty-bound to issue a further warning. I know, Mr Edge, that all the rest of my men are not of the type to be concerned by what may or may not happen to them should they break a law or two and offend diplomatic principles?'

Edge had been rolling a cigarette and now he struck a match on the butt of his holstered Colt to light it as the rider on the far side of the wagon looked pointedly toward him.

'The major's asked you a question, Mr Edge!' Breslin snapped imperiously.

'I would say Mr Edge is well aware of that, Ben,' Cutler said evenly.

'And I guess you're well aware of how I'll answer it, Major?' the half-breed countered on a trickle of exhaled tobacco smoke.

Cutler looked long and hard at Edge, his lips pursed and his dead eyes giving no clue to his frame of mind. Then admitted as he turned to gaze toward their destination: 'Yes. In many ways I think you are much like the rest of the men who have rallied to my call.'

'The kind who'll do just about anythin' for a buck, I'm thinkin'!' Ben Breslin growled sourly, a newly-acquired resentment acting to nullify his earlier good-humoured liking for the half-breed's style.

Edge answered in a wry tone: 'I guess there aren't too many laws I'm not ready to share my situation with right now, Sergeant.'

'Uh?' Breslin grunted while Cutler ignored the exchange.

Edge said shortly: 'Broke.'

5

SAN JUAN had once been to the Mexican state of Sonora what Devlin was to the United States Territory of Arizona. A military fort. But no community had been established outside its gates in the manner of Crooked Creek.

Perhaps because such a development had been forbidden. Or maybe because nobody not under military rule would choose to put down roots in such a wretchedly desolate area. Or it could have been that *El Alcazar de San Juan* had been abandoned by the army and left to crumble toward ruin before a civilian population had time to settle within its shadow.

The fort came into view shortly after the trail and arroyo swung to the south again after curving eastward to cut through the fold of two hills. The terrain here was in the form of a long valley, both flanks of which were a series of irregular humps that mostly had fans of scree spilled down between them. None of the near barren slopes rose to more than a hundred and fifty feet, and the San Juan fort was sited on a ledge some fifty feet up the slope of the eastern valley head, its gated front wall facing north. Above the fort the degree of slope became much steeper and the name of the place was inscribed with infills of red sandstone packed into lettering gouged out of the grey granite.

Dust disturbed by the winds of other, less still days had obliterated some sections of the lettering. And the wood-smoke that had first been visible above the hill crests now to the north of the wagon and two outriders—it drifted lazily up from within the fort walls—made it additionally difficult to discern the name that had been so arduously set into the steep grade.

Jefferson Cutler had been watching Edge for several moments after they were in a position to see the fort. And on his face was an expression of strangely anxious expectancy: like he was eager to have an opinion he would respect and was worried it would not agree with how he felt.

But it was Breslin who spoke first. Started to explain: 'This piece of country is called the Valley of San Juan, Mr Edge. What it says up there above the——'

'I've got it, Sergeant,' the half-breed broke in as he shifted his glinting-eyed gaze away from the fort to peer down the valley into the heat-shimmered distance. Noted that the trail virtually petered out from lack of use just a short way beyond the slope with the fort on it.

'It was built by penal labour over twenty years ago, I'm given to understand,' Cutler said. 'I suppose the prisoners who were the most serious offenders had the task of cutting the name into solid rock.'

Edge glanced again at the six-feet high lettering as he arced away his cigarette butt and said: 'Looks like it was a job that cost a lot of blood, sweat and tears. Major.'

'I'm thinkin' that won't amount to nothin' like it'll cost them Apaches in the long run, uh Major?' Breslin growled.

They were immediately below the fort now, turning to head up a hoofprinted and wheel-rutted pathway between the trail and the gateway. Which was close enough to see how the walls of the fort had been pitted by gunfire. And certainly a great deal of the shooting had not been so long ago. For the dust-powdered ground over a wide area was littered with spent shellcases. None of them tarnished. All glinting in the glaringly bright sunlight of mid-morning.

'That's for the future, Ben,' Cutler responded, not failing to notice that Edge was paying close attention to many factors about his surroundings while he apparently

49

looked about himself with just casual interest. 'Almost without a single exception, Mr Edge, my men are lone wolves. Or they have formed partnerships. Thus are they unfamiliar with working as a group: a team. We have staged training exercises. Much in the manner the regular army trains its raw recruits.'

'And most of the men have learned from it, I'm thinkin',' Breslin hurried to put in, becoming increasingly disgruntled by the way in which Cutler was talking to Edge as an equal to the apparent exclusion of himself. 'Am I right, Major?'

'Some have, Ben,' Cutler allowed, detached.

The half-breed nodded and said: 'I guess this place is too far from anyplace else for all that shooting to bring the local Federales riding in to check up?'

Cutler showed a rare smile that bared his very white teeth but failed to inject a spark of life into his almost yellow eyes. He said with a hint of triumph: '*El Alcazar de San Juan* was not built simply to break the backs and spirits of men sentenced to penal servitude, Mr Edge. Then abandoned. It was intended for use as a military establishment in the defence of Mexico against the United States in the event of aggression. But this area of the border is a cause of dispute between the two nations. It has been so for some considerable length of time. And until agreement can be reached we are in what may be termed a no man's land.' His smile seemed for a fleeting moment to flicker with a hint of humour: that sounded as cynicism in his voice when he drew the silver-handled black cane from the rifle boot on his saddle and waved it in a negligent encompassing gesture. 'Though why any man, leave alone a country, should wish to lay claim to such a Godforsaken stretch of land I can't imagine. Except for the pure greed of ownership, perhaps?'

His tone and expression became grim once more as he reined in his mount, along with Edge, as Breslin rolled the wagon to a halt, before the firmly closed double gates. 'But for the moment, the land and the fortress serve my purpose. And I have to admit, Mr Edge, I rather hope the question of ownership of them remains higher on the list of diplomatic priorities than the matter we discussed earlier.'

He seemed about to amplify this, but suddenly realised there was no need. Nor time, anyway. For the two gates began to swing into the fort, creaking on ungreased hinges. And one of the men grimacing with the effort of dragging open a gate accused grouchily:

'You took your friggin' time, Breslin! My belly's gettin' to friggin' forget what it feels like to have grub in it!'

'Parkin, you could go without food for a month and still be carrying too much fat!' Cutler snapped.

The complaining man, who was maybe a little thicker around the belly and neck than Cutler, eyed his glowering employer with the same jaundiced look as he had given to Breslin. But was persuaded to swallow back an embittered response: either by Cutler's penetrating gaze or the sudden recollection of how much he was getting paid each day to be respectful.

'That's it, friend, eat them words you had in mind to speak and maybe they'll hold you until I've fixed break-fast!' Breslin growled as Cutler heeled his mount forward into the fort. The skinny, tall, scar-faced man who had opened the second gate threw up a sloppy salute, and this was acknowledged with a touch of the cane handle to the major's Stetson brim. While Breslin indicated the half-breed with a hooked thumb and announced: 'A new man, Parkin. Name of Edge. Show him to some quarters. One of the spaces left by Billy Burroughs and Emmet ought to be fine, I'm thinkin'.'

He flicked the reins to start the team moving. And like Cutler who had already gone from sight behind the wall to the right, gave not a backward glance toward Edge as the wagon trundled across the compound.

'Decision time, new man,' Parkin growled, still dis-gruntled with his world in general of which the half-breed was now a part. 'You havin' second thoughts or do you want to be like all the rest of us? Abandon hope and enter here?'

'Don't mind Parkin, Edge,' the second man on gate duty

said. 'When he's not griping he's trying to be funny. Nobody's sure which is the worst.'

The half-breed urged his horse into the fort as he acknowledged what the two men had said with a barely perceptible nod of his head. And then remained in the saddle of the again stationery gelding, raking his impassive gaze over his surroundings as the gates were dragged closed again and secured with a plank dropped into a pair of rusted iron brackets.

El Alcazar de San Juan was built to much the same pattern as most other military forts Edge had been in, the majority of them north of the border. A pattern that had doubtless been established far back in history when one group of men had first felt the need to protect themselves and their possessions from the belligerent aquisitiveness of another group. There had been refinements down the years to ring minor changes. And the building materials depended in the main upon what was readily available locally.

The twenty-feet high walls of this fort were of adobe that had been weathered to various shades of cream and brown. The walls were some four feet thick and enclosed an area of about three hundred by four hundred feet—the side walls a third as long again as those at the front and rear. The topmost four feet of all the walls were less thick, so that walkways were formed. Factory-made ladders that looked to be brand new against the twenty-year-old fabric of the fort gave access to the walkways at each corner.

The largest area within the compound was a drill square, and there were flat-roofed adobe, timber or stone buildings on three sides of this. A barracks and a mess and stables on the east side. Officers' quarters, the magazine, the sutler's store—its façade above the doorway and window painted with the Mexican term *vivandero*—and the guardhouse on the west side. Under the rear, north wall, were buildings that accommodated the quartermaster's store, the office of the fort's commander and what could well have been married quarters for a few privileged officers.

'You know something, Parkin?'

'I know lotsa things, Fish,' the ill-humoured man growled as Edge completed his initial survey of the fort and swung down out of his saddle.

'If wit was shit, you'd never be troubled by constipation,' the man with a scar on his chin retorted. And gave vent to an oddly girlish giggle before he explained his attempt at a joke. 'On account of you don't possess any wit!'

Parkin disproved this by growling: 'If wit was shit I figure *I* wouldn't half suffer with constipation.' Then, while Fish frowned as he struggled to work out the hidden meaning of the cryptic response, Parkin asked of Edge without any change of tone: 'You seen enough for now?'

'Sure. If you two fellers have gotten over the attacks of verbal diarrhea.'

'Oh, hell, another guy who figures he's a comedian,' Parkin groaned and shot a pointed glance at Fish before he jerked his head to indicate the way they were going to go and then set off.

He and Fish were both in their mid-thirties. They were similarly outfitted in far from new but hard-wearing Western style clothing. Both wore gunbelts with unfancy Colt revolvers jutting from their tied down holsters. Each had also had easy access to a Winchester rifle while they stood sentry duty at the fort entrance—the weapons now leaned against the wall at either side of the gateway. As the flabby Parkin led Edge across the drill square toward the adobe-built stable block, the skinny Fish resumed his watch on the terrain to the north of the fort by means of a spy hole in one of the gates.

The only other man carrying out sentry duty was patrolling the west and south walls, ambling lethargically along the walkways and occasionally raising to his eyes the binoculars that were hung around his neck on a cord. He looked a good deal older than Parkin and Fish. But maybe it was his heavy black beard that created a mistaken impression at a distance. Or it could be his gait, sluggish in the energy-sapping high heat.

Another horse was being led by the reins across the drill

square. The dapple grey gelding of Jefferson Cutler. A lithe-looking young man with hard eyes that looked older than his twenty some years had charge of the horse now that Cutler had gone into his quarters. Edge was aware of the hard eyes appraising him. Knew, also, that he was the subject of a disjointed study by the two forty-year-old men who were helping Breslin to unload the flatbed and tote the supplies into the cookhouse at one end of the mess. Their eyes were as hard as those of the youngster. He sensed other watchers, too. Men who were in the barrack block that had a roofed porch running the entire length of its façade. At this time in the morning the windows out of which the men peered at the newcomer were in deep shadow.

'Reckon you know you're gettin' the once over from most of the boys, Edge,' Parkin said, his tone empty of any kind of feeling now that the exchanges with Breslin and Fish were part of the forgotten past.

'It's only natural, feller.'

The fat man nodded without turning his head. 'What I was goin' to say to you. They don't mean nothin' by it. Old stagers figurin' to get their first measure of the new man.'

'Sure.'

'Some of them maybe recognisin' you, could be? Eager to hear your name in case they can recollect hearin' that. It's happened a few times that old enemies have met up here, Edge. But old scores are bein' pushed to the back of the oven. You likely to have any old scores to settle with the kinda guys you're gonna be beddin' down with?'

'No sweat,' the half-breed replied evenly as Parkin directed a quizzical glance over his shoulder at him.

'I reckon you were in Crooked Creek at the time Rankinn and Wade took care of the trouble Billy Burroughs and Emmet thought they had with each other?'

'Yeah.'

'And either the major or Ben Breslin told you how——'

54

'Feller?' Edge cut in, his tone weary.

'Yeah?'

They had reached the doorway of the stable and come to a halt.

'I never volunteer for anything unless I know the ground rules. Even when I'm as broke as I am now.'

'Okay,' Parkin acknowledged, his mood suddenly close to petulance. Then, abruptly, he snapped a finger and thumb: extended the finger toward Edge as enlightenment showed on his face. 'Hey, I bet you're the guy that Wade and Rankinn met up with in town after——'

'You got it, feller,' the half-breed confirmed as the kid with eyes older than his years made it a group of three plus two horses out front of the stable.

'Ethan Rankinn said you came on like a guy who reckoned he knew it all . . . His words, not mine!'

Edge responded evenly to the fast-spoken interpolation: 'Figure you do so much talking you have to borrow from others sometimes, feller.'

A man in the barracks guffawed.

Parkin growled: 'Yeah, another guy who reckons he's a friggin' comedian. There's the stable. That's the barracks. Reckon you don't need me no more?'

'Much obliged,' Edge said and Parkin turned on his heels and headed back across the drill square toward the gateway.

The kid said cheerlessly: 'I'm the duty wrangler today. Take care of your mount unless you're set on doin' it for yourself?'

'Much obliged,' the half-breed said again, and handed his reins to the kid.

'Name's Madonna. Mike Madonna from Missouri.'

'Edge. Nothing else. From Iowa, way back.'

'I never heard of you, Edge.'

'Nor me you, Madonna. Parkin figures that has to be good around here.'

'P.D. Parkin is right,' the young man said in his melancholy monotone. 'Sometimes he's that. But Wade and Rankinn have heard of you. They're real mad at you for rubbin' them up the wrong way, so you'd better watch out for them.'

He made to go into the stable.

Edge glanced around the fort and asked: 'Where do I watch out for them right now?'

'Right now they're out range ridin'. Took off with Harry Bean and Phil Turner soon as they'd hauled in the corpses and set a couple of men to buryin' them. It wasn't their turn to do the range ridin' but they were so mad at what happened with you, they just had to get on and do somethin'. Instead of sittin' around here stewin'.'

'A patrol, Madonna!' Ben Breslin yelled irritably along the length of the barrack from the cookhouse doorway to the entrance of the stable. 'A patrol is what those men are on! Lookin' for Indian sign! They ain't ridin' no damn range watchin' over a herd of cattle, boy! Those four men are out on patrol, you hear!'

'Oh no they ain't, Sergeant!' the bearded sentry yelled down from the corner where the south and west walls joined. 'On account of all four of them boys are headin' in! And they got them a prisoner, looks like!'

'Indian, Collins?' Breslin bellowed.

The sentry swung around and raised the glasses to his eyes. Peered southwards for stretched seconds before he reported into the suddenly tense silence that was compressed within the walls of the fort: 'I reckon white is what he used to be, Sergeant!'

'Talk sense, man!' Breslin thundered as Jefferson Cutler appeared at the doorway of his quarters across the square.

'Or suffer for your stupidity!' the major supplemented, his voice as ice cold as the expression on his face.

'He's a white man!' Collins confirmed, his manner unaffected by the threat. Then added: 'Under a whole lot of black and blue!'

'You'll give me a report, Sergeant!' Cutler snapped.

'Surely will, sir!' Breslin acknowledged as Cutler turned and stepped back into his quarters. Altered his tone to rap out harshly: 'You men finish unloading the supplies!

Madonna, see to those horses! Parkin, Fish, get them gates open!'

He started to stride purposefully across the square toward the gateway. And some men emerged from the barrack, to align themselves in the shade of the porch roof. A dozen, in various states of undress from resting in the barrack. Few of them even cast glances in the direction of Edge, their curiosity about the newcomer temporarily displaced by interest in the beaten-up prisoner being brought to the fort. Then one of them, who was closest to the half-breed, said without shifting his scornful gaze away from Breslin:

'He sure can holler, can't he?'

'Never have come across a sergeant who couldn't feller.'

Another man muttered sourly: 'They don't have to have no brains. Just so long as they can yell loud enough. Cause a normal man to bust a gut.'

The squat-framed, almost bald man who had opened the exchange said: 'I reckon the more brainless a guy is, the more friggin' noise he makes.'

'That's right, Walsh,' a third man growled. 'The reason you talk so much, uh?'

There was a ripple of half-hearted laughter along the line as hoofbeats could be heard out beyond the open gateway. Walsh was unperturbed to be the butt of sardonic humour. Said:

'You notice how so many army sergeants are Irish? Anyone know what they call a guy with brains in Ireland?'

Nobody supplied the cue for which he angled and he shrugged as he answered his own question in a dull tone: 'A tourist.'

There was no laughter at this, as all attention was focussed on the gateway where five riders had come to a halt. Four were in process of swinging down from their saddles. The fifth man could not yet dismount, for his wrists were tied to his saddlehorn.

'Guess Lew Collins was almost right,' the nearly bald man muttered. 'A greaser's more of a white than an Injun. I guess.'

Edge said flatly: 'Walsh, that your name?'

The total coldness in the half-breed's voice caused most of the men in the shade of the porch roof to look toward him. And they were in time to see his narrowed eyes shift their gaze from the activity at the gateway to lock on the perplexed face of Walsh.

'That's right. What of it?' He was ready to be angry.

'You know what they call somebody who insults my father's race after I've told them I don't like to hear it?'

Perplexity became anxiety in back of the thin veneer of a scowl. He parted his thin lips to reveal gritted teeth, but before he could vent a rasping response, Edge told him:

'Dead.'

6

MEN WHO had started to return their attention toward the fort entrance now snapped their heads around to direct intrigued double-takes at the half-breed. Men who were hard-eyed and mostly unshaven. In an age group from thirty to something over forty. Life-toughened men who lived by the gun. Thus, even those who had been taking their ease in the barrack garbed only in pants, barefooted and naked above the waist, had taken the time to buckle on their gunbelts before filing outside.

Such men were seldom surprised, which was witnessed by their mere survival. For they would have entered into and emerged from countless life or death situations. And in so doing they had learned how to spot the first signs of imminent danger. Prided themselves on this art that enabled them to pre-empt the threatening moves of an enemy. To surprise him even before he was ready to spring his own surprise.

But the half-breed had fooled them on this glaringly bright, blisteringly hot morning. They had seen him at first impression as a soft-talking, slow-moving, even-tempered, down-on-his-luck drifter lured to *El Alcazar de San Juan* by the carrot of high pay. Which explained why Wade and Rankinn were so all-fired mad after their run-in with him at Crooked Creek. He was the kind of frontier riding bum either one of those gunslingers could have handled between two slugs of whiskey without letting go of the bottle—if Jefferson Cutler hadn't happened to get to town at the wrong moment.

That was probably what they had thought about the new

recruit until he caused them to re-assess their opinions of him: by the manner in which he uttered that single word—*dead*. And now it was almost possible for Edge to see behind their faces into their changing minds as they completed their double-takes and gained their second impressions. He shared in much that made them the kind of men they had become. It could be that Wade and Rankinn were lucky to escape their trouble with him. The warning he had just issued to Walsh was meant to be registered by all of them. And from the way he stood there out in the brilliant sunshine . . . And by the total impassiveness of his expression . . . Add the stance and the look to the tone of his voice . . . The total came out at a man who did not voice idle threats. Who was ready, here and now to prove the point. Unconcerned that he was a newly arrived stranger facing up to a dozen gunmen who were instinctively formed into an alliance from being together for so long.

As many of the men before the barrack block resumed their interest in the group at the gateway, one of those who was bare chested said with a sneer:

'Mister, you must have a death wish.'

'Feller,' Edge drawled, 'I gave up on wishes when I found out Santa Claus didn't exist.'

Breslin yelled above the harsh grating sound of the ungreased hinges as the gates where swung closed: 'Madonna! Get over here and take care of the horses! You men at the barrack! Get yourselves properly dressed and fall in! Maloney! Pick a firin' squad!'

The youngster emerged from the stable and the men began to go back into the barrack. Nobody moved with the degree of urgency which Breslin's orders would have inspired had they been regular soldiers in a regular army. But some of the men uttered rasping, low-toned complaints in the time-honoured manner of the lower ranks duty bound to obey higher authority.

The half-breed was eyeing the prisoner whose hands were being released from the saddle horn by the blond-haired Wade. And did not realise the bare-chested man

60

who had made the death wish comment was the last man to re-enter the barrack until he growled:

'I'm Maloney, Edge. You're first man on the firin' squad. So best you go get that Winchester I saw in your saddle boot, uh?'

Then he went out of sight through the doorway. And yelled out four more names against the hubbub of noise of the men cursing and griping as they dressed. Ed Walsh, Pierce Browning, Drew Peppard and Sam Stafford.

Edge had returned his narrow-eyed gaze to the activity just inside the gateway by then, where the prisoner was being dragged rather than helped down from his saddle. This as Breslin whirled and marched toward the open doorway that gave on to Cutler's quarters.

When the Mexican was on the ground, his wrists still securely tied in front of him, nobody offered him support in staying on his feet. But he managed alone and became rock steady, his legs braced apart, after several moments of swaying and staggering within a restricted area among the horses. He started to sway again after Madonna had taken up the reins of all five horses and led them away. But by squeezing his eyes tightly closed and concentrating an effort of will toward the single desire of staying erect to the exclusion of all else, he was able to remain rigidly on his feet. The amount of resolution this required showed plainly on his face. And outside of a grimace that had briefly contorted his features at Breslin's mention of a firing squad, this was the only sign the prisoner had shown of his emotions since he was brought in through the gateway.

Or maybe it was just that his face was so cruelly marked by the vicious beating that only the most emphatic of expressions, of feelings so strong as terror or near super-human effort, could be seen at the distance over which the half-breed viewed the man. A man of close to forty. An inch or two under six feet tall and solidly built without an ounce of excess fat on his frame. Attired in black pants and vest and white shirt and riding boots with ornate spurs. All of his sweat- and blood-stained clothing decorated in Mexican style. The hat he should surely have started out with under the blistering sun had been lost since his capture.

Perhaps he had been a handsome man before the beating cut and bruised his face, which was now swollen and crusted by congealed blood into a mask of ugliness, dully coloured in shades of yellow and purple and rusty red. Sweat trickled down over his punished face and dripped on to his chest like blood had done earlier.

Then Madonna blocked off the half-breed's line of sight as he drew near to the stable entrance, the five horses in tow, and offered: 'You want me to bring out your rifle to you, Edge? Jack Maloney ain't a man you wanna get on the wrong side of. You've got enough enemies here already.'

'Much obliged,' Edge said. And when the youngster moved on by he found his attention diverted from the doomed prisoner who was finding it increasingly difficult to win the struggle to stay on his feet, head held high. Was drawn to look toward the group of men comprised of Wade, Rankinn, Parkin and Fish and the two he had heard named as Phil Turner and Harry Bean.

All of them were peering across the square at him while the short and fat P.D. Parkin spoke fast with animated arm gestures.

'You hear what the Mexican is supposed to have done?' the half-breed asked of Madonna as the scowling young man advanced only as far as the stable threshold to thrust the Winchester out at Edge.

'No chance,' came the growling response. 'Just because I'm the youngest gun around here, I get treated like a little kid. Nobody tells me anythin'. They'll find out soon enough I ain't no little kid.'

He spat forcefully, the globule of saliva arcing several feet out over the dusty drill square. Then, as Edge took the rifle and canted it to his shoulder, Madonna withdrew quickly into the stable. Like he was anxious not to be seen by Breslin who stepped out of the doorway of Cutler's quarters and bellowed:

'Get the lead out, you men! Maloney, you better have picked that squad! Prisoner and escort, march over here!'

His voice rang out sharp and clear and seemed to be somehow strangely amplified by a quality not unlike an echo within the confines of the fort walls. Ben Breslin, an old army man, was revelling in this situation. And this was not only heard in his voice. It could also be plainly seen in his upright bearing and the way he swung his arms as he marched to a spot immediately out front of the commanding officer's office. Where he seemed on the verge of stamping through a drill manual about-face. But then he seemed to sense this would be an empty and foolish gesture of a man briefly lost in memories of the long gone past. And when he turned around without any hint of military precision, his round face beneath the kepi's visor expressed grimacing disdain for what he saw. Two groups of men—the smaller approaching from the gateway and the other coming away from the barrack—were ambling across the drill square without either the urgency or the mien he wanted of them. But when he shot a concerned glance toward Cutler who stood at the doorway of his quarters, the major gestured with his cane for Breslin to stay calm.

'Firin' squad's all picked out, Breslin,' Maloney said. 'That's me and the new——'

'I don't care who they are, friend!' Breslin snapped, glaring at the forty-year-old with unruly black hair and a straggly moustache, who looked even bigger and broader now that he was fully dressed. 'Just form them up in the first rank, Maloney! Wade, bring the prisoner over here! Rest of you men, fall in! Ranks of six behind Mahoney's squad!'

The men shuffled sluggishly into the formation Breslin required, many of them cursing softly. Edge found himself between Maloney at one end of the front rank and the squat Ed Walsh. Along with Browning, Peppard and Stafford they were the only men on parade who carried rifles. But everyone packed a sixgun in a holster: and some even had matched revolvers in twin holsters.

Except for the prisoner who did not even wear a gunbelt. He alone deported himself to some extent like a soldier on parade: but this was obviously not an impression he was trying to create. He moved with such strained rigidity because only thus was he able to keep himself from collapsing to the ground. And in his desperate circumstances the ability to prevent himself from falling was the last straw of dignity to which he could cling. He continued to hold on to this, gazing blankly ahead out of eyes almost forced closed by bruising, while his wrists were untied from in front of him: then were bound again at his back to trap him against one of the two posts that flanked the porch of the office doorway, supporting the roof.

This was no more than twenty feet distant from the men in the front rank of the dishevelled parade. And everyone could hear the blond-haired Wade cursing as he worked at untying the tight knot in the length of rope. Then could see from the viciousness of his gestures that he pulled the rope even tighter still as he made the prisoner fast to the post. But the punished Mexican did not even grimace, and it was Wade who expressed a soured mood when Breslin ordered him to join the parade. Then it was unnecessary for the man with chevrons on his civilian shirt to report to Cutler that all was ready for him. For the man whose money had assembled this private army at the fort had started to stride across the drill square as soon as Wade had completed his chore. But Breslin felt compelled to snap out:

'Parade, attention!'

A little dust rose as a few booted feet were scraped across the parched ground. And a few disparaging words were rasped. But before Breslin, face redder than ever, could give vent to the fury rising inside him, Jefferson Cutler commanded:

'Stand easy, men!'

'Shit, it's friggin' hot and I forgot to bring my hat,' somebody in the rear rank complained.

'An order to stand easy does not grant permission to talk!' Cutler barked as he reached the front of the parade and came to a halt at one side of the prisoner while Breslin stood on the other side, nodding his approval. 'That man will dig the grave for the prisoner!'

The puffed and blood encrusted lips of the Mexican twitched in response to this. And maybe he began to sweat more than before. But everyone was sweating freely at this time of day, close to noon, for there was no shade upon the area where the men stood.

'Noted, Major,' Breslin acknowledged with the ghost of a smile.

Cutler then turned his back on the parade and stepped directly in front of the prisoner, bringing up the cane to cant it to his right shoulder. From his manner it was obvious that he was scrutinising the man from head to toe and then back up again. A process that took perhaps five seconds, during which the breathing of men and the sounds of horses moving in the stable were the only noises against the hot silence. Then:

'I am given to understand that you are Raul Escobar?'

The Mexican had maintained his straight-ahead stare while Cutler surveyed him, which meant that his eyes were almost on a level with those of the American who was only slightly the taller of the two. But it was a moot point whether the punished man actually saw the one who had condemned him to death. He was not so detached from his dire circumstances that he failed to hear, though. For he swallowed and rasped:

'*Si, senor.*'

Cutler slowly moved his cane away from his shoulder and rested its ferruled tip on the shoulder of Escobar. Asked: 'I am given to understand that you speak my language, Mr Escobar?'

'*Si.* . . that is correct.'

Cutler sharply raised the cane from where it rested and swung it to the side. To tap it against the left bruised cheek of the prisoner rather than to strike a blow. But the Mexican instinctively rolled his head to the right as he was instructed:

'Then speak it, Mr Escobar.'

'I do not understand why I have been beaten and brought——'

Cutler hit the man's face a little harder this time and this at last extracted a reaction from the dark eyes of the prisoner. Which were suddenly focussed upon the dead eyes of his tormentor to express a mixture of hatred and terror.

'You will speak when I tell you, Mr Escobar. In answer to the questions I will put to you.'

The cane was allowed to rest on the shoulder of the Mexican again, as Jefferson Cutler spoke in the same even-toned manner he had adopted from the outset of the interrogation. Probably, Edge guessed, the expression on his face was a match for the voice. Neither of them revealing to Escobar the extent of the strain that held Cutler in an ever tightening grip— unless the prisoner was sufficiently perceptive within his state of despair to recognise that the grey-haired man was not just sweating from the heat of near midday. The back of his shirt, a freshly laundered one he had changed into since returning from town, had progressively darkened with the damp of perspiration since he turned to face the Mexican.

'You are a Government agent, Mr Escobar?'

'No! No, I work for a railroad company!'

'You hid, I am given to understand, from the patrol of my men? Mistakenly believing they had failed to see you?'

'*Si* . . . yes, I hid when I saw the four riders. This is bad country. There are Indians here. And bandits. Even Federales who will sometimes shoot first and then ask the questions.'

Cutler nodded several times after Raul Escobar began to list the kind of people who inhabited the country to the south of *El Alcazar de San Juan*. Then said: 'I may not command the most disciplined force ever mustered, Mr Escobar . . .' He cast a disdainful glower over his shoulder at the group of men aligned in three ranks of six, then returned his attention to the prisoner to conclude: 'But at least *they* leave an enemy with enough life to answer *their* questions.' He vented a short, brittle laugh.

Escobar rasped: 'They beat me, but I can tell them nothing but the truth.'

Then he flinched: rolled his head to the side, away from where the cane rested on his shoulder. Obviously seeing in

66

Cutler's face a signal that the evenness of his tone and earlier lack of expression had been a sham. And, just for a moment, Ben Breslin looked as concerned as the prisoner at what he read in the major's features: seemed about to lunge forward and yell a warning in an attempt to restrain the enraged man.

But Cutler was not yet about to kill Escobar in a homicidal frenzy. He withdrew the cane. Took a double handed grip on it, at the handle and tip. Stepped up close enough to his victim so that he was able to raise the cane and press the black malacca against the throat of the helpless man: under the chin and above the Adam's apple. Pushed it hard enough into the pulsing, sweat-sticky flesh to force a gasp of shock and pain from Escobar, but did not block his windpipe.

'You are a liar, you pathetic, snivelling sonofabitch!' he accused, cold anger ringing in every snarled syllable as the heat of his emotions pumped out more sweat to darken his shirt. 'I know a little of your language. Enough to tell you I know you are speaking *caca de toro,* uh? Bullshit, Escobar! You are a Mexican government agent! And a bad one! Not even smart enough to have a reasonable lie ready in the event you were caught! The San Juan Valley is disputed territory. There's no railroad company that would send out a man to survey this part of the country. Not even smart enough either to know when you've been spotted. A dumb fool who ducks into a hole in the ground! And cowers there waiting for my men to go away! Do you think I am the same kind of dumb fool you are? What do you think I am Escobar? Do you and your government think I don't know I can't set out to do what I plan without attracting official attention from both sides of the border? You should simply have admitted who and what you are, Escobar! Saved yourself a great deal of grief and pain!'

He suddenly backed off from the man: who sagged forward now, breathless and suffering a greater degree of pain and humiliation. Held partially upright by the way his wrists were lashed together behind the post. No longer able to hold his head erect.

Then Cutler began to beat him with the cane. First to one side of the head, than the other. Causing him to cry out in agony as each blow of the wood thudded with a sickening sound into his face or skull.

Then Raul Escobar dropped to his knees. And began to whimper rather than to cry out as each sideways blow of the cane swung him by turns to left and right. Not just his head now. His whole body, on the pivots of his knees, as the parched and dust powdered ground to either side of him became darkened with splashed blood.

Cutler began to breathe noisily. And then Edge became aware of some of the men beside and in back of him giving vent to similar sounds. But whereas the man administering the beating was unwittingly signalling his over-exertion, many of the witnesses to his sadism were held in the grip of a frenetic blood lust: hardly able to keep themselves from screaming excited encouragement at Cutler. Others were as implacable as the half-breed himself as they watched the cruel ending of a man's life: as silent as they were expressionless. A few—the scar-faced Dale Fish over by the gates, Drew Pearson who walked with a slight limp and others whose names were unknown to Edge—were so revolted by what was happening they had to turn their horror-filled eyes away. Ben Breslin was in no position to do this.

'Major!' he yelled, no longer able to contain his shock at what he saw. But he did not lunge forward. By an effort of will remained rooted to the spot. 'Major Cutler, I'm thinkin'——'

Jefferson Cutler suddenly curtailed the vicious beating and stepped back from his helpless, softly moaning victim. Looked away from Escobar and at Breslin. Then his frame shuddered with a kind of overwhelming sigh that threatened to drain him of the final reserves of strength left to him after the beating.

'As you were, Sergeant!' Cutler snapped. And for a fraction of a second Breslin looked afraid for his own safety. Before the man he held in such high regard fastened a more secure grip on his composure and added evenly: 'It's all right. You can dismiss the men.'

'But, Major! I was told to fix up a firin' squad!' Jack Maloney sounded like a spoiled child who had not gotten what he had asked for on his birthday.

'Parade——' Breslin yelled as a prelude to carrying out Cutler's order.

But Cutler whirled around to face the ranks of men who mostly showed the same expressions as when they had watched the beating. While Cutler, the front of his shirt as wet with sweat as the back and stained, too, with spots of his victim's blood, for a stretched second looked to be on the verge of white hot anger again. But he controlled the impulse, or perhaps felt the rage swamped by the enormity of another emotion. Which could have been shame. But Edge was unsure of this. For the yellowish-brown dead eyes of the man came to humiliated life for just a part of a second. Then Jefferson Cutler was coldly in command of himself and his highly paid army again. Growled:

'Maloney! You'll join Driver on the burial detail! The two of you will get to it immediately after the dismiss. Sergeant, dismiss the men.'

Edge sensed the resentment rising within the big man at his side. But, once more, the knowledge of how much money was on the line bought compliance from a man unused to taking orders. And like many of the others, Maloney confined the expression of his resentment to a scowl and muttered curses as Breslin snapped:

'Parade, dismiss!'

And Cutler killed Raul Escobar. Executed the prisoner with such speed of action that most of the men failed to see it. As he had turned toward the man with the bloodied head again, he had resumed a two-handed grip on the cane. Then had twisted one wrist and thrown his arms apart. The silver handle came away from the wooden length of the cane. But not just the handle. For below its hilt there was a thin blade. Some nine inches long, tapered to a point. The Mexican had forced his head up when Cutler named the two men who were to dig his grave. But his eyes were curtained by blood and so he could not have seen the weapon glinting in the noon sunlight. More blood from the wounds at either side of his head had masked many of the bruises and earlier lacerations that marked his face. And so it was impossible to read any expression on the mutilated features. His mouth opened and closed once, but whether to curse his torturer, plead for deliverance of give vent to his anguish could not be heard. For just a faint gurgling sound emerged. And then he was dead. After Cutler dropped into a half-crouch, drew back his right hand and thrust it powerfully forward. To plunge the stiletto blade into Escobar's chest. Left of centre.

'Sonofabitch,' Ed Walsh growled.

'Did you see that?' the squint-eyed Driver gasped rhetorically.

Breslin turned in time to see Cutler withdraw the blade from the heart of the Mexican who was still spasming through his death throes. This act of jerking the knife free of the flesh separated by no more than a second and a half from when the now straightening man had detached it from the shiny black cane.

For no reason—no command was spoken nor signalled—the men's reactions to the killing thrust were suddenly curtailed. And they were as still as they were silent. So that Jefferson Cutler's words, uttered at the level of a reflective whisper, reached many ears:

'My two girls took longer to die than you, Escobar.'

'Major?' Breslin said, concerned.

Cutler looked up from the now inert form of the dead man crumpled at the foot of the porch roof post. And as he shifted his gaze from Breslin to some of the men who continued to watch him, he was briefly perplexed: then perturbed as he realised he had spoken aloud the mitigating excuse meant only for a corpse past caring. He seemed ready to be angry again, but only at himself for the lapse in concentration that had caused him to drop his guard. Then, an instant later, he had controlled all outward signs of this. Told Breslin to carry on and whirled to start back toward his quarters in a striding gait. The wooden section of the cane in one hand and the knife in the other: seemingly unwilling to re-connect the two parts until the blade had been wiped clean of blood.

With a jerk of his head, Breslin signalled for Maloney and Driver to attend to the dead man. They had cut his bonds and were starting to lift his limp form between them, as Cutler slammed the door of his quarters behind him. Which was when P.D. Parkin yelled across the drill square which was now almost clear of men:

'Hey, Breslin! We already missed breakfast! How long we gotta wait for the next—'

'Tend to your duty, friend!' His voice was at its loudest and he sounded more Irish than ever as he bellowed the order at the short, fat man who leaned against one of the gates. And it was obvious that Parkin had set himself up as the target for a depthless anger that was melded from a whole range of powerful emotions that had erupted in a turmoil within Ben Breslin's mind. But then he was able to force himself back under control, as he wrenched his gaze away from the suddenly anxious man at the gate. And he stared with an embittered scowl at the corpse slung between the two reluctant undertakers as he fisted and unclenched his hands. Muttered: 'Holy Mary Mother of God . . . What kind of men can think of their bellies right after . . .' He shook his head morosely.

'The hungry kind,' Driver growled. And spat.

Maloney added sourly: 'And here's one for sure'll be a whole lot hungrier after he's planted this corpse.'

They carried their sagging burden toward the south west corner of the compound heading for the gap between the quartermaster's store and the *vivandero*. And Breslin caught up with Edge who was angling toward the stable and perhaps spoke aloud his thoughts, unware and uncaring who was his sounding board as he continued in the same vein as before:

'Just what manner of evil men has the Devil sent here?'

He swung his head, mildly startled, when Edge responded evenly:

'The kind who'll do just about anything for ten bucks a day, feller.'

Breslin looked poised to growl an embittered counter. But then pursed his lips as he took his empty pipe from a shirt pocket and clenched the stem between his near toothless gums. Nodded and allowed: 'You're right, friend. I'm thinkin' it's a brotherhood of mean-hearted killers we wanted and we got.'

Edge drawled: 'Headed up by a feller who's real able with a cane.'

7

BRESLIN WAS either too pre-occupied with pondering the immediate past or not familiar enough with the story of the Garden of Eden to understand the half-breed's sardonic reference to Cutler's killing of Escobar. The two men moved on side by side for another few paces, then went their separate ways. The man in the kepi toward the cookhouse, the chimney of which was now billowing more smoke than ever, and the man with the rifle sloped to his shoulder heading into the stable, where Mike Madonna was rubbing down Raul Escobar's horse. All the other animals that had been ridden into the fort this morning were already enstalled with feed and water and their coats had been curried clean of trail dust and sweat lather.

Stalls were ranged down each side of the building, longer than it was broad, and an aisle separated them. Saddles were hung from pegs outside every occupied stall. He spotted his gelding from the threshold of the stable, a third of the way along. Then saw his bedroll on a table near where Madonna was working on the dead man's mount just inside the building.

'I took care of him as well as I know how, Edge,' the mean-eyed youngster assured without pausing in his chore. 'Same as I do any job I'm given. Wherever it is.'

'Place smells cleaner and looks better run than a lot of town liveries where I've bedded down a horse, feller.'

'It was like that when I got detailed to wrangler duty this mornin',' Madonna said, anxious not to claim undue credit.

'That gimpy Drew Peppard had the duty yesterday. And P.D. Parkin the day before that. P.D. said as how Ethan Rankinn who was wrangler before him left the place in a real mess. Hey, that was really somethin', wasn't it? The way the major beat up on that guy and then stuck him with the knife?'

Edge did a double-take at the young man who had started to talk more quickly, the words rattling out and sometimes running into each other: like Madonna was afraid of the silence a pause would bring. And he saw that he was working on the horse with faster, harder actions, too. Which almost, but not quite, served to disguise the fact that he was having trouble to keep from trembling.

'Something you'd never seen before, feller?' the half-breed suggested evenly.

'A guy get killed? Hell, no. Look, you're supposed to keep your weapons in the barrack. And ain't no beddin' nor personal stuff like that supplied. So I took your bed-roll off of your saddle. If you wanna go pick out a space in the barrack . . ? Or maybe you want some stuff outta your saddlebags?'

More fast talk while he pointedly avoided looking at Edge. Anxious for the half-breed to leave before the final shreds of his assumed toughness were stripped away by the vivid memory of Raul Escobar's killing.

'Obliged, but for now I guess I'll just need the bedroll,' Edge told Madonna as he crossed to the table.

Hooves clattered and wheelrims rattled as the flatbed wagon was moved from the doorway of the cookhouse to that of the stable. Then a man growled as the rig came to a halt:

'Two more for you, Mad Mike. Sure is a busy day, boy.'

'Bastard,' Madonna rasped softly, his anger with the man outside acting to calm his jangling nerves.

'Is it the Mad Mike or the boy that needles you?' Edge asked as he picked up his bedroll and started back for the door.

'What's the difference to you?' the younger snarled, hard eyed again. Looking like the kind who never shuddered, unless from the cold.

'You said it,' Edge remained. 'I've already made more than enough enemies in this place.'

'Mad Mike!' Madonna snapped as the half-breed reached the threshold and paused. 'It was what some lousy newspaper up in Kansas called me one time. After three women got shot up real bad in a bank hold up. But it wasn't me did the shootin'. It was the guy I was runnin' with then. And he got killed pretty soon after that, so wasn't no-one left to prove he was the trigger-happy mad guy. That bastard Wade saw a wanted poster on me once. So he started in to call me the name. And most of the other guys around here do the same. Ain't no reason why you gotta be any different from all of them, Edge!'

'You have your opinions and I'll have mine, Madonna,' the half-breed told him as he stepped away from the doorway and moved along the front of the barrack, the porch roof of which cast little shade now that the sun was beyond its noon peak and beginning its slow slide down the western side of the cloudless sky.

For the first stint of afternoon duty, Lew Collins had been replaced by Ed Walsh who now ambled back and forth along the walkway of the west wall. And Dale Fish and P.D. Parkin had been relieved by Drew Peppard and the freckle-faced Pierce Browning at the gateway sentry positions. Nobody else was outside in the blistering heat. Most were back in the barrack, sprawled out on their cots as they waited for the call to eat. Which would not be long in coming if the strong fragrance of chili in the woodsmoke from the cookhouse chimney was anything to go by.

Within the barrack the cooler air was rancid with sweat on unwashed flesh and body-soiled clothing and bedding too far removed from the last laundering. Also permeating the atmosphere was a lacing of bad breath and belly gas. The aroma of tobacco smoke from several cigarettes and cigars and two pipes was barely detectable.

'Any one that ain't got blankets on it,' the flabby, under five and a half feet tall Parkin growled lethargically from where he sat on a cot, legs splayed out in front of him and back against the wall immediately opposite the only doorway of the building. He was stripped to the waist and was slowly scratching with both hands in the thick matting of hair on his heavily fleshed chest.

This was the only stirring of activity within the barrack that was a little longer and about the same width as the stable. The door was at a midway point in the façade and there were four unglazed windows at either side of the entrance, shutters folded back on the inside. There were no windows in the rear or end walls. Wooden cots without head or foot boards were aligned along the front and rear walls. Sixty in all. About twenty of these were taken and most of them were occupied when Edge entered the building. Just Parkin and two other men had claimed cots against the rear wall, directly across from the doorway. The rest were spread on cots to either side of the threshold, with the only vacant places at each far end.

At either end were stoves, unlit in the heat of the day. Midway down to each end from the doorway, in the centre of the ten-feet wide aisle between the rows of cots, were pine tables each with two attendant straight-backed, hard-seated chairs. A kerosene lamp hung from the ceiling above each table. There were no closets or lockers between the beds. Weapons and all items of clothing not being worn as the men took their ease were stowed beneath the cots. And none of the ten-dollar-a-day hired guns had seen fit to personalise his restricted living area with a picture or a crucifix or some other kind of keepsake on the wall above his head.

The harelipped Rankinn said from where he lay on his back on the cot immediately to one side of the doorway: 'The further down the room the better, far as I'm concerned.'

He had just completed a search of one of his nostrils and now he wiped his exploratory finger on the blankets beneath him.

Edge drawled: 'When what concerns you concerns me, I'll let you know, feller.'

'A time and a place, old buddy,' the blond haired Ray Wade muttered sleepily from where he was sprawled out, belly down, on the cot at the other side of the doorway. 'And this ain't neither of those for the unfinished business we got with our pal.'

Some men who had stirred themselves to look toward the doorway with mild interest after Rankinn issued the challenge now resumed previous attitudes, knowing from past experience that Rankinn always went along with what Wade said. And Edge moved on into the barrack, to claim the first available cot against the rear wall to the right, next to one that was unoccupied at the moment. As he dropped his bedroll on to the straw-filled mattress a man across the room drawled:

'Ain't a bad choice, Edge. You're next to Jack Maloney and he ain't much of a snorer.'

'Hope you ain't much of one either,' another man growled. 'We got enough noisy sleepers in this joint already.'

Harry Bean said defensively: 'Shit, a guy ain't responsible for what he does when he's sleepin'.'

'Some of them around here when they're awake, too.'

No one was prepared to take issue with whoever made this comment and the desultory talk came to an end. This as Edge finished stowing his eating utensils beneath the cot with his rifle and then lay down on his unfurled blankets: tipped his hat forward over his face and interlocked his hands behind his neck.

The inside of the Stetson smelled of his own sweat, strongly enough to mask most of the other bad odours in the room. The series of low sounds made by the other men as they took their ease, along with the occasional noise that intruded from outside the barrack was easy on his ears. And had it not been for the uncomfortable emptiness of his belly Edge thought he might well have been able to drift into a shallow sleep.

Then, maybe fifteen minutes after he had stretched out on the cot, a clamorous din of metal striking metal shattered the malodorous peace. And as booted feet were swung off cots to thud to the dirt floor, the clanging ended and Breslin bellowed:

'Grub up, come and get it, friends!'

The bare-chested P.D. Parkin led the hurried exodus from the barrack, most of the men pausing only to gather up their eating utensils before they made haste to answer the call to the cookhouse. Dale Fish, so emaciatedly thin he looked in urgent need of food, was one of those who waited for the rush to be over before he started out of the barrack. He said as he gestured for the half-breed to go through the doorway ahead of him:

'Get ready for a real treat, mister. Ben Breslin sure can cook good. I ain't never tasted food so good since my Ma passed away.'

Maloney and Driver approached the barrack, sweaty and dirty and ill-humoured from the gravedigging chore. The squint-eyed Driver growled:

'If you figure that mush Breslin serves up is good, your Ma must've been the worst——'

Fish came to a sudden halt and whirled around, his skinny face heavy with anger. And spittle sprayed from his mouth above his scarred jaw as he challenged: 'You'd better not insult my mother, you pile of shit!'

Driver checked his move to go into the barrack. Turned more slowly than had Fish. And all the irritable resentment he had felt for the burying of Raul Escobar was directed at the skinny man. First with a scowl. Then in words. 'Big fan of your momma, were you?' he mocked. 'Loved you're momma, did you?'

'Shut your filthy mouth, you shit!'

'Don't you call me names, you little runt of a mother-f——'

Driver started toward Fish, both big hands clenched into fists. But the bigger and stronger Maloney took a hold of one upper arm of the squint-eyed man and gestured with his head across the drill square. And everyone looked in the direction he indicated: saw Jefferson Cutler peering out of the window of his quarters.

'You want to be in the next grave dug under the south wall?' Maloney asked, shifting his gaze between Driver and Fish.

'Aw, shit!' Driver growled, wrenched free of Maloney's grasp and swung around to go into the barrack.

'What you are, sure enough,' Dale Fish rasped after him.

Maloney sneered: 'It's what you make a lot of us want to do, the way you run off at the mouth about your old lady like she was some kinda——'

Breslin thrust his head out of a window in the front of the mess hall to demand: 'What's the trouble down there?'

'There ain't no trouble,' Maloney answered. And stared hard at Fish and Edge for backing.

'Me and John Driver got different opinions about the food you cook, Sergeant,' the scowling scar-faced man said.

'And I settled their differences,' Maloney added.

Edge said, with a glance across at the window from which Cutler had withdrawn: 'Kept the shit from hitting the fan.'

8

THE BOWL of chili that Edge ate in the reasonably clean mess hall was good-tasting and along with a hunk of sourdough bread it filled him. There was nothing wrong with the coffee, either. But then he was no connoisseur of fine food: and if he were, a heap of ground beef flavoured strongly with chili peppers was not the kind of meal he would have chosen as the basis for passing judgment.

In common with most of the men who ate without talking at two runs of tables with bench seating at each side, he ate the food cooked by Breslin for the same reason as he always ate any meal: because he was hungry, and it was just a bonus when the food turned out to be good.

When the eating was over most of the full-bellied men were in a better humour. And there were just a few token gripes from such men as Rankinn and Driver and Parkin as Breslin detailed afternoon duties. Duties which invested the fort with a semblance of the military order for which it had been built. Edge was assigned to a four man patrol along with Sam Stafford, P.D. Parkin and Lew Collins. As they saddled up their mounts, other men were detailed to KP and the rest were ordered to prepare for target practice from the walkways on the wall tops.

As the four-man patrol mounted and started across the drill square amid the rest of the unhurried activity, Edge sensed watching eyes. And surreptitiously he pinpointed two men who appeared to be more suspiciously interested in the patrol than in anything else that was happening in the fort. Cutler was peering out of the window of his quarters, holding the wrong end of the cane with his left hand and gently striking it against his right palm. While the slightly-built form of Dale Fish was discernible on the threshold of the fort commander's office. Breslin had detailed him to clean out the office, but until the patrol neared the gates that were swung open for the riders, Fish remained in the shaded doorway. Fingering the scar on his jaw as he pretended to be just mildly interested in every aspect of the activity on the square.

Then the bearded Collins, who was nominally in command of the patrol, led the way out of the fort. And the half-breed allowed to himself that he could well have been over-sensitive for those few moments before the gates folded closed behind him. Perhaps Jefferson Cutler was enduring a period of remorse as he gazed out upon a piece of sun baked ground where he had tortured and killed a man: and just happened to be looking with apparent mistrust toward the patrol whenever Edge cast a glance in his direction. Similarly, Dale Fish could well have been merely goldbricking. It had been impossible to see his face in the shadows beyond the threshold: so his expression could have been vacant instead of heavy with suspicion which was how the half-breed had visualised it in his mind.

Outside the fort, on the downslope from the gateway to the trail, the air was as hot and dry as that within the adobe-walled compound. But it smelled a whole lot fresher. And maybe it felt freer . . ? Edge vented a low, short grunt which was the only outward sign he gave of the conscious effort required to halt this line of thought. He was not normally given to flights of fancy. Probably a half dozen or more men had paid more than passing interest in the patrol as it prepared to leave the fort. Looking no more pointedly at Edge than any of the other riders. With resentment or envy rather than a darker emotion: wishing it was they who had been detailed to take a ride away from the claustrophobic atmosphere of *El Alcazar de San Juan*.

'Hey, will you guys look at that!' Ed Walsh yelled as the

four riders reached the foot of the slope and turned to go down the trail to the south. 'We got us some movin' targets to make the shootin' a little more fun today!'

The heads and shoulders of a dozen or so men could be seen at the top of the west wall that commanded a view directly down on to the trail. But only one of them had a rifle stock pressed to his shoulder, barrel angled over the wall so that the muzzle was trained on the four slow-moving riders.

'Friggin' idiot,' the fat Parkin growled.

Sam Stafford, who was a buck-toothed and hollow-cheeked ugly man of about thirty confined his response to a sneering look of contempt in the direction of the fort. Lew Collins spat in the opposite direction and drew an arm across his beard to wipe off some of the saliva that was caught in it. None of them aware for perhaps two seconds that Edge had reined in his mount: then reached forward with a hand to rest it on the stock of the Winchester jutting out of the saddle boot.

They halted their horses then, and looked back at the half-breed. At such close quarters were able to clearly see the mixture of ice cold anger and searing hatred that resulted in a kind of mirthless grin on the lean, dark brown face: drawing back the thin lips from the startlingly white teeth and cracking the eyes to the narrowest of glittering slits.

'Sonofabitch,' Parkin rasped.

'Shit,' Stafford added, and looked ready to gallop his horse clear of the danger area.

'You'd better not——' Collins began to order thickly at the same time as the other two men were venting their nervous reactions. But curtailed it when another man's voice began to sound at the top of the wall.

'Walsh, I'm thinkin' you're the biggest fool that the good Lord ever created! Edge——if you take that rifle out of the bucket I'll order every man to open fire on you!'

The red headed man came into sight shortly after he started to rap out the hard-toned words. And he moved along the walkway from the top of the ladder at the north west corner of the fort. Stopped alongside Walsh, and by turns switched his glowering gaze between the squat, balding man and the tall half-breed astride his horse below. He said nothing, and after he had clenched the stem of his pipe between his almost toothless gums, the silence that his Irish accented voice had effected seemed strangely harsher and more menacing.

Edge ended it: 'Walsh?'

'Damnit, I wasn't gonna fire nor nothin'!' the frightened-sounding man said to Breslin as he dragged the Winchester back off the top of the wall.

'And the rest of you!' Edge went on. 'The same with guns aimed at me as with insults to Mexicans! A man does it after I've warned him not to, the thing gets to be a matter of life or death!' He withdrew his hand from the rifle, took up the reins and prepared to heel his gelding forward as he lowered his voice to say, the killer grin sliding off his face: 'I'm ready when you fellers are.'

'We're all shit scared, Edge!' Ethan Rankinn yelled down, his challenging voice heavy with sarcasm.

'You know somethin', mister?' Parkin muttered with a frown.

Up on the wall, Breslin roared: 'You know what I am, friend? I'm friggin' up to here with you men actin' like a crowd of squabblin' schoolbrats! I'm wishin' I had got out to see the major a whole lot sooner that I did! So I could've seen you bunch of crazy fools before he hired you! And now I'm wishin' there was time enough left so me and the major could fire the whole friggin' lot of you! And start to enlist the kind of men who'll do like they're told for the kind of money bein' paid without all the time . . .'

The patrol had started along the trail again and a widening distance in combination with the clop of hooves acted to mask the angry tones of Breslin who had wrenched the pipe from his mouth and begun to stride up and down the walkway. And Parkin held off from replying to his own rhetorical query until the enraged voice reached down as nothing more than a drone.

'I don't reckon I ever met up with a guy so all fired ready to start trouble than you, Edge.'

'Wrong, feller,' the half-breed countered as he took out the makings. 'Trouble is something I try to avoid. Figure everyone around here now knows what it is that riles me.'

'I'm with P.D.,' Stafford said with a slow shake of his head. 'Beats me how you've got away with it so long, mister. Mouthin' off about your own private rules and how you'll kill any man that don't abide by them. We ain't no bunch of squabblin' brats like Breslin just said. Why, if the pay wasn't so high to make us fall in with the army-like way Cutler likes things run, you'd be dead by now. In my opinion.'

'Damn right,' Parkin agreed as Edge remained impassive while he completed rolling the cigarette, then lit it with a match struck on the butt of his holstered Colt. 'I'm ready to stake money on somethin'. Back there at the fort—and includin' us out here—I reckon there's more killers and outlaws and all around mean-assed bastards than ever's been in one place before. Outside of a territorial prison, maybe? Schoolkids, that Ben Breslin called us! Why, if it wasn't for that ten bucks a day . . .' He suddenly realised he was wandering away from his point. Directed a penetrating gaze at the half-breed and concluded: 'If I was you, when this job is over I'd high tail it outta here. Real fast. Before some of the guys remember there ain't no more big bucks bein' paid to keep them from makin' you prove you ain't all talk.'

'Much obliged for the advice,' Edge said evenly.

'Which you don't need?' Lew Collins growled.

'About as much as anybody needs this crazy patrol crap,' Stafford said sourly.

This before a barrage of gunfire shattered the tranquility of the hot, still air beyond the reach of the sounds of slow-moving horses and the low-voiced talk of the riders. When all four men looked back along the trail, in time to see drifting black powder smoke and small clouds of billowing dust. The smoke from the side of the hill that hid the fort from sight in this direction and the dust moving just above the ground in the area where the bullets impacted.

'Or needs shootin' practise!' Parkin rasped. 'All this crazy play-actin' at bein' friggin' soldiers.'

'We can all shoot good as we have to,' Stafford said, nodding and scowling. 'And ain't no Apaches gonna come sneakin' up on us through this patch of badlands. Why, I bet that Escobar guy that Cutler killed wasn't no government agent. Was a railroad man like he said. And them guys just hauled him for somethin' to do. Break the friggin' monotony of these lousy patrols.'

'And if Cutler gets them Gatlin' guns like it's said he's waitin' for, won't be any need for no fancy shootin',' Parkin came back.

They were still close enough to the fort for a second fusillade of rifle fire to make talking an effort. And there was a pause until the din was curtailed. Then Collins asked:

'You pick up anythin' in town on that story, Edge?'

'No, feller.'

Stafford said: 'Rumour is he's got a deal with the army at Fort Devlin.'

'Nah,' Parkin dismissed. 'Jefferson Cutler ain't dumb enough to figure he can get a couple of Gatlin' guns off the United States army. They're comin' up outta Mexican is what I heard.'

'He sure goes to see that Crispin guy who's the big cheese at Devlin enough times,' Stafford reminded.

'That's to find out if he can talk his way into gettin' some help on the level from the cavalry to find his missus,' Collins said. And looked at Edge with much the same kind of expression as when he spoke to Parkin or Stafford, apparently having decided to accept the half-breed as an equal. 'You rode in with Breslin and Cutler from Crooked Creek, mister. They say anythin' to each other that the rest of us should maybe know about?'

'There's no word yet that anybody outside of the bunch he's hired is going to help him. About all, feller.'

Collins scowled. 'Figured as much from how he's been since he got back from town. The way he beat up on that Mexican and stuck him with the fancy knife. Like he was real mad at somethin'.'

'Maybe mad the Gatlin' guns ain't got here yet?' Stafford suggested.

The scowl darkened above the black beard as Collins countered: 'More likely he ain't sure we got the firepower to do what he has in mind. And maybe he's right to get nervy about that. You picked up anythin' about what Jefferson Cutler really has it in mind to do, Edge?'

'Hunt Apaches and hope to find his wife while he's doing it is how I heard it.'

Collins spat and again had to wipe some spilled spit out of his beard. 'Yeah, that's how this thing started out, mister. But the longer we been together, more set Cutler gets on wipin' out the entire Apache nation. Instead of just the bunch of renegades that hit his place. And some of us ain't so sure ten bucks a day is enough to have that many Apaches mad at us.'

'That's right,' Stafford agreed, nodding vigorously. 'That fort back there ain't no Alamo and we ain't the same kind as Crockett or Travis. And the only one of us with a cause is Cutler. I know that was a Mexican war, but——'

'Nor that asshole crawler Ben Breslin,' Parkin added.

Edge drawled: 'Figure that if the job doesn't come up to expectations, you can always leave.'

Stafford made a throaty sound of disgust, then complained: 'The only time I made more than ten bucks a day this easy was when I was holdin' up stages. And the time I served in state prison when they caught up with me wasn't easy at all.'

'What I'm friggin' sayin', Sam,' Collins growled. 'Goin's soft as a baby's rear end now. But the lead's gonna start flyin' for real pretty soon. And the way Cutler is gettin' to be so jumpy . . . Well, it's makin' me and some others just as friggin' jumpy.'

'Don't be such a Goddamn party pooper, Lew!' P.D.

Parkin rasped. 'Like our new man says, when we figure it's time the money ain't good enough for the work we have to do, we up and pull out. No quittin' notice to serve, far as I'm concerned.'

'Try it, you jerk,' Collins countered bitterly. 'And it's my opinion you'll get paid off with a bullet in your back. Same as Emmet and Billy Burroughs.'

The fat man pulled a face that was perhaps intended to convey his disdain for what was said. But then his fleshy body was shaken by a shudder, like he was cold for a stretched second in the blazing sunlight that poured down upon the quartet of riders and the barren piece of country through which they moved. He said nothing and the talking was not resumed for more than a full minute, even though the latest burst of gunfire from back up the trail was too muffled by distance to have masked even a whisper. Then Parkin suggested:

'Hey, maybe Cutler's so jittery on account of he ain't been able to figure out who the spy is?'

Collins scowled at Parkin, then looked quizzically at Edge, as if he expected a query. When he drew just an impassive gaze through the drifting smoke of the cigarette angled from a side of the half-breed's mouth, he explained anyway: 'Our bunch sure is like a regular army in one way, mister. Rumours get started out of nowhere and from nothin'. Newest one is that the major thinks we got a United States lawman at the fort. Passes on information about what we're doin' to that Schroder guy that's the sheriff in Crooked Creek. And he gets it to someplace else, higher up. Real crazy.'

'Crazy is what the guy must be goin' if he's really at the fort,' Stafford muttered. Then laughed harshly before he added: 'On account of ain't nothin' happened yet that's worth tellin' anyone about.'

There was agreement in the silence that greeted this expression of opinion. This time, nobody spoke for upwards of two minutes. And it was Parkin again who ended the pause.

'I reckon we've come far enough, Lew. Ain't no sense in

bustin' our butts ridin' any further south. Just means a longer ride on back to the fort.'

Collins glanced over his shoulder, checking that they were out of sight of *El Alcazar de San Juan* that was something over a half mile to the north. Then he allowed, with misgivings: 'Okay, if you guys are ready to risk it. Sure is hot as hell out here.'

He and then the other two directed questioning looks at Edge, who responded with a quizzical raising of his eyebrows after he had arced his cigarette butt to the dusty ground.

Parkin gestured with an arm to encompass the trail ahead and the almost featureless hillsides that flanked it. Asked: 'What's the friggin' point, mister? I noticed you been watchin' every which way since we started out. You reckon we're gonna see anythin' except the same kinda emptiness if we keep on headin' out this way?'

'Yeah, let's rest up here for an hour or so,' Stafford agreed. 'And head for home.'

Collins, still ready to fall in with the wishes of Parkin and Stafford, remained unconvinced it was the right thing to do. Said: 'And hope that Cutler don't find out we ain't done what Breslin ordered us to do? No tellin' what'll happen to us. We all know the way Ray Wade and that Rankinn sidekick of his blasted them two guys in town for not doin' like they was told.'

'You're the top hand, feller,' Edge replied as Collins peered levelly at him, maybe seeking support.

'Uh?' the black bearded man grunted.

'Far as I'm concerned this is an army of sorts I'm in,' the half-breed told him. 'Breslin assigned you to lead this patrol. If any man on it doesn't obey your orders, it's him that's wrong. Even if he thinks you gave the wrong orders.'

'Thanks for frig all!' Collins snarled.

'So what we gonna do, Lew?' Stafford asked, bewildered, as he prepared to rein his horse to a halt.

'What Breslin told us, damnit!' He spat so forcefully this time that all the saliva cleared the bristles of his beard. 'Bust our friggin' butts lookin' for friggin' Injuns and Federales that ain't there! P.D. and Edge, you head up——'

'They're there, feller,' the half-breed cut in as Collins threw out his left arm to point up the rising ground beyond the dry wash to the east.

'I'm top hand, like you just said, mister!' Collins raged. 'So don't you argue with me about . . .'

He, Parkin and Stafford all abruptly ended their intense study of the impassively set face of Edge. Realised they had misinterpreted what he had said. And all three turned their heads to peer in the same direction as the narrowed, glittering slits of his eyes. To where three men astride horses were skylined on the crest of the rise to the west. About a quarter mile away. Close enough to be plainly seen against the heat shimmer which curtained the sky behind them. A trio of braves, certainly Apaches in this area, wearing leggings and waistcoats, cuffs and headbands that supported single eagle feathers: and probably with weapons belts around their waists. Hardy looking ponies under them. Rifles held in single-handed grips, resting across their thighs. No warpaint.

The dust raised by the unshod hooves of the animals when they were reined to a halt on the ridge was still settling when Stafford gasped: 'He's right! And we got them savages out-numbered!'

Then he thudded his spurred heels into the flanks of his gelding as he wrenched over the reins to command an instant galloping turn. Next his teeth-crowded mouth gaped open to give vent to a bellow of elation as he jerked the rifle out of his saddle boot.

'Shit, come on!' Parkin yelled against the thudding of hooves and the voice of Stafford as the ugly man shrieked incomprehensible words. But then he checked his move to chase off up the hillside in the wake of Stafford. After he had directed a stunned double-take at Edge and Collins. Then he did as they had done, and reined in his mount.

'Sam!' the bearded man roared, cupping his hands into a bullhorn at his mouth.

'What the frig's wrong?' Parkin demanded, an expression that was a mixture of anger and bewilderment on his fleshy features. Not needing to raise his voice against the diminishing sound of shod hooves at a gallop.

'I figure Stafford is,' Edge replied evenly, not shifting his unblinking gaze away from one particular point on the ridge until the three braves had calmly wheeled their ponies and ridden at a walk out of sight. Then he made a fast survey of the closest horizons on all sides. And said as he was doing so: 'Three against four doesn't add up, feller. Not this close.'

Stafford was looking back over his shoulder now, brandishing his rifle above his head. Obviously experiencing a higher level of excitement as he urged the three men on the trail to join him in chasing the fleeing braves.

Parkin forced out from a constricted throat: 'Oh, sweet God in heaven.'

Collins bellowed Stafford's given name, and seemed on the point of spurring his mount forward. But was able to halt the move as the exhilarated man halfway to the ridge wrenched his head around to face front again. In time to see six figures on the skyline. All Apache braves. On foot, so that their aimed rifles could be held rock steady: to their shoulders and their cheeks.

Stafford fired one shot. Maybe for effect. Or perhaps his finger squeezed the trigger as part of his terrified reaction to a first glimpse of the line of Indians. It was also questionable whether he purposely abandoned his rifle or it slipped from his trembling hand. This before he jerked on the reins to drive his mount into a tight turn. Which the horse completed but he did not. For the Apaches exploded their rifles at him, the spurts of muzzle smoke seen by the men on the trail before the crackle of the reports reached down the slope to their ears. And the ugly Sam Stafford was falling to the ground by then. Knocked sideways out of his saddle by the impact of the bullets against and into his flesh. Just for a moment it seemed that his right foot was trapped in a stirrup and he would be dragged back down by the bolting horse. But then

90

man and animal became separated and the man was an inert heap on the incline, dust raised by the pumping hooves settling on to his body where it clung to the blood-oozing wounds.

The killing rifles were single shot weapons. Springfields, maybe, Edge thought as he and Collins and Parkin watched them reloaded. The fat man's throat was still tightened by shock and his rasping voice was barely audible when he asked:

'Lew, you think we oughta get the hell away from here?' Then he shuddered, in much the same way as before. On this occasion reacting to a second fusillade of gunfire—the line of Apaches loosing six bullets into the unfeeling sky. After which they turned with the same arrogant lack of haste as the mounted braves earlier and ambled out of sight. And Parkin snarled, anger starting to displace fear and shock as Stafford's horse came close enough for the blood on the saddle to be clearly seen: 'What the frig was that for?'

Collins answered tautly: 'How the frig should I know?'

Edge offered: 'I read it that they ain't ready to kill us yet. Unless we're as ready as Sam Stafford to die. And they ain't short of ammunition.'

'Makes sense,' Collins muttered, the tension beginning to drain out of him as the riderless horse slowed to come to a snorting halt close by its own kind.

'Sam sure didn't show any, chasin' off the way he done,' Parkin muttered.

'How'd you know there was more of them Injuns up there?' the bearded man asked, genuinely intrigued and maybe displaying a hint of new-found respect for the half-breed.

'I didn't know, feller. I just made an educated guess.'

His fleshy face set in an embittered scowl, Parkin sneered: 'Like they say, education is a wonderful thing, mister. Just bad luck for Sam he never had your advantages, uh?'

Edge rasped the back of a hand over the half day's growth of bristles on his jaw-line as he directed a bleak, glinting-eyed gaze at the corpse of Stafford, as awesomely still as the parched ground upon which it was sprawled. And responded flatly: 'Maybe he just didn't pay as much attention as I did, feller. Don't they say also that a little knowledge is a dangerous thing?'

9

A SMALL group of riders had started out along the trail from *El Alcazar de San Juan* in response to the two volleys of rifle shots fired by the Apaches. But the half dozen men reined in their mounts and waited under the west wall of the fort when they saw the patrol heading back north.

Three riders in line abreast at the front with the fourth behind—the news of a casualty was relayed to the fort by a shouting voice when the returning patrol was close enough for the slumped body to be seen over the saddle of the horse on a lead line. Then, when the survivors were close enough to be recognised, they were within earshot of the news shouted to the top of the wall by Ben Breslin that it was Stafford who had been hit.

Jefferson Cutler was among the men aligned on the wall and his commanding tones rang out above the babble of questions yelled down at the trail as the two groups of riders came together: 'Sergeant, have the patrol report to me inside the post!' He snapped his head from side to side as the anxious queries were silenced. And selected the two men closest to him, stabbed the silver handle of his cane at each of them as he ordered: 'You and you, burial detail for the dead man.'

Then he swung around and started for the nearest ladder to the ground, perhaps unaware that one of the men he had picked was the squint eyed John Driver: who had earlier drawn the gravedigging chore for Raul Escobar. In any event, Driver confined his reaction to the unfairness of the work load to a resentful scowl. Probably gave outlet to his seething indignation with curses and vicious use of the shovel into the ground as he worked alongside Harry Bean on the rapidly expanding burial area out back of the buildings beneath the fort's south wall. But whatever sounds the two of them made were masked by the clatter of hooves and the thud of booted feet as the returning riders came in through the gateway and swung out of their saddles: surrounded by the men who had climbed down from the wall walkways.

Breslin snapped orders: 'Parkin, take the body back to where it's to be buried! Madonna, get over here and attend to the mounts! You men, get them gates closed! Walsh, for frig sake get back up on the west wall! Rest of you men——'

'Okay, Sergeant,' Cutler broke in, his voice lacking volume but heavily laden with grim forcefulness. His yellow-brown eyes stayed dead looking as he flicked their gaze between Edge and Collins when he continued: 'The post is secured. All the men have a right to hear what took place. Which of you will supply the report?'

'Collins had charge, Major,' Breslin rapped out. And was briefly disconcerted by the fleeting expression of angry impatience Cutler directed at him. For he was obviously unused to being on the receiving end of such a tacit censure from this man he held in high esteem.

As the black-bearded man began to give an at first disjointed account of the run-in with the Apaches— perturbed at being in the unfamiliar position of having such a large audience of listeners gathered around him—Edge moved out of the centre of the group. He still had hold of the reins of his gelding and it was his intention to take care of his own horse himself while the youthful Madonna was busy attending to the other animals. Then, as he drew close to the stable doorway, he found himself distracted into doing a double-take toward the gap between the quarter-master's store and the *vivandero* at the south west corner of the compound. Where a wagon was parked, its tailgate facing out on to the drill square. It was a Conestoga with its hooped canvas cover in place and the rear flaps tightly fastened together at the centre. By ducking down as he walked he was able to see the legs of a four horse team that was still in the traces.

The half-breed thought immediately of the Gatling guns which Cutler was rumoured to be expecting. Had they been delivered from the north while the patrol was out on the south trail? Or maybe the Conestoga was about to leave the fort. Just because he had not seen the rig before did not have to mean it was a new feature within the walls of *El Alcazar de San Juan*. It could have been parked out of sight behind one of the buildings aligned on three sides of the compound.

'You guys weren't the only ones to have some trouble, Edge,' the hard-eyed Mike Madonna broke in on the half-breed's irresolute line of thought.

Edge uttered a questioning grunt as he glanced at the lithely framed youngster who was hitching horses to the rail outside the stable: so he could take care of one at a time inside.

'Women,' Madonna answered. And nodded toward the wagon. 'Guess you ain't never heard of no whoremaster named Howie Beach? Like a lot of the guys here?'

Edge looked again at Madonna after making another fast study of the Conestoga in light of what he had just been told about it. And started to ask: 'Cutler let a feller bring whores into——'

But Jefferson Cutler himself unwittingly interrupted the half-breed's evenly spoken query, raising his grim-toned voice so that it reached to all sides of the compound after Lew Collins had completed his report: 'All right! Anybody didn't hear what happened, Sam Stafford was shot dead by Apaches! There were six of them for certain! Perhaps nine! Perhaps many more who did not show themselves! This on the same day that we captured an agent of the Mexican government in the vicinity of the post! There can be no doubt! The time for training is almost over! I refuse to give permission for those women to remain within the confines of this post!'

There were perhaps three stretched seconds of uneasy silence in the wake of the man's oratory. Then a

95

female voice complained from within the tightly enclosed Conestoga:

'Hell, Howie! We come all this lousy way for nothin'!'

This triggered a babble of talk from the group of men close to the centre of the drill square. But Cutler did not come to an angry halt midway between the ill-humoured gathering and the threshold of his quarters until Ethan Rankinn challenged:

'So you can fight your own friggin' fight, pal!'

The silence these sourly spoken words brought about was tenser: but lasted less than half as long. Breslin ended it as Cutler began to slowly swing into an about face.

'You're talkin' mutiny, I'm thinkin', friend.'

Cutler was looking at the men with his dead eyes again, slapping the handle of his cane into an open palm. His distinguished features were set into a strangely uncaring expression: like he was a mere spectator at a competitive event, the outcome of which was utterly immaterial to him.

'No, Major,' Ray Wade interceded, his tone evenly pitched—reasoning. 'I figure my old buddy here is talkin' as close to sense as he ever gets.'

Somebody vented a hollow laugh, which was curtailed by a sharp cry: as if irritation with the man's amusement had resulted in a covert but painful blow being struck.

'I'm thinkin' this could be gettin' close to conspiracy to incite mut——' Breslin began to growl.

'Let the man say his piece, Ben,' Cutler cut in, matching the tone of the blond-headed half of the Wade-Rankinn partnership.

'Appreciate it, Major. You got yourself a bunch of high-livin', red-blooded men out here in the middle of nowhere. And it's pay day again. Been a long, hot week again. And if Howie and his girls didn't show up, then I figure most of us would just have gone on into Crooked Creek and done us a little drinkin'. Same as on other pay days. But if you allow Howie and his girls to stick around, well I figure a whole lot of men will stay close to the post, too?'

The querying tone with which he completed his point

was accompanied by a side-to-side movement of his head as he looked for agreement from the others. This drew a murmuring of assent intermingled with a few louder whistles and catcalls. Then Jefferson Cutler brought quietness to the sun-bright drill square again when he raised his cane in unspoken request. And asked:

'What if I confined you men to the post?'

'Just try it,' somebody said. Maybe Jack Maloney.

Another man warned: 'We'll take only so much of this army stuff, Cutler!'

Yet another started out in a placating tone: 'We'll kill Apaches for you, Major . . .' And then sounded a note of warning: 'But we ain't gonna live like friggin' monks. Not when good old Howie Beach had brought us out some fine stuff to——'

'Just give me the word, Major!' Breslin snarled.

Cutler, who was apart from the group and the only man whose face and actions were plain to see by Edge and Madonna out front of the stable, had remained impassive as he swung his cane with one hand against the other. Now his calmly spoken words were in keeping with the rest of his demeanour as he asked: 'What word is that, Ben? If I am not mistaken I think I could call to mind a dozen words to convey my feelings for what is happening here this afternoon. But to what avail with regard to our purpose? I have a proposition to put to you men.'

He moved his grey-haired head, to scan every face with his lifeless eyes. Then gave a curt nod in acknowledgement of the tacit agreement he had read. Offered: 'I will permit the whores and their procurer to pitch camp outside the walls of the post. Close enough to be under our protection in the event of an attack. Not within my sight unless I elect to see them. If this arrangement is not satisfactory the employment of every last man here is terminated. That is all. Dismiss the men, Sergeant.'

So saying, the icily calm man executed a more formal about face and headed into his quarters at a gait that was closer to a march step than a walk. And the cluster of men who had never on this occasion fallen into any semblance of a military formation on the drill square at least remained silent until the door was slammed closed behind Jefferson Cutler. All of them perhaps perceptive enough to know that the man paying big bucks for ready gun hands was not playing a game of bluff. That he had just gone as far as he was prepared to go: and not just on this issue. If he was forced into a corner on any other point that went against his grain, there was no more slack line trailing away from his temperament. It was taut to breaking strain.

A muttering of talk began and the underlying tone sounded sullen. Until the flaps at the rear of the Conestoga were abruptly wrenched apart and a raven-haired woman of uncertain age showed her over-painted face and over-blown bosom above the tailgate to yell:

'Hey, you guys! We'll go along with what the boss man says! And Howie says to give us thirty minutes to set up the store and lay out the goods!'

This produced a raucous cheer from the men. Then the wagon was jolted into forward motion. Went from sight around the rear of the quartermaster's store. Reappeared between this building and that which housed the commander's office. This as Breslin yelled at the duty sentries to open the gates. An order that was obeyed just in time. For the slightly built old-timer who was driving the wagon demanded a gallop from the team, his long and angular face set in a grin of pure pleasure as he steered the rig at full speed across the square. Men who would soon be paying for the company of his whores scattered from out of the path of the hurtling wagon, some cursing but most laughing. And the gates, difficult to move on their dry hinges, were not fully open and allowed just sufficient clearance when the straining team hauled their pitching and yawing burden out over the threshold of *El Alcazar de San Juan.*

Dust from beneath the pumping hooves and the spinning wheels all but concealed the rear of the wagon and the three figures who showed themselves above the tailgate, arms waving and mouths gaped wide to shriek laughter and encouragement: lost under the din of the rig's headlong progress.

Then the gates were swung closed and the dust began to settle. And the sun was obscured by one of many white clouds that were starting to mar the smooth expanse of pale blueness that had been the borderland sky until early afternoon.

Madonna shook his head and frowned as he restarted the exchange with Edge out front of the stable: 'Never figured it to end with the major backin' down. Way things was shapin' after that Beach guy and his women got let into the post, looked like there was gonna be some fightin' here. Maybe a killin'. Hell of a lot of bad mouthin'.'

Edge nodded as he led his gelding through the stable doorway ahead of the younger man with the piebald mount of Lew Collins. This as Breslin snarled out orders to send the men back to whatever duties had occupied them before the wagonload of whores and the shots that signalled the death of Stafford provided disruptive interruptions.

'But he's a real smart guy, that Jefferson Cutler, is what I think,' Madonna went on as he and the half-breed began to unsaddle the respective horses. 'I figured at the start he could have give a couple of the guys a hard time and sent the women packin'. And got away with it. But after the Apaches killed Sam Stafford . . . Well, I don't know . . .'

'Life's too short to miss out on too many of the good things, even at the best of times, kid,' the half-breed supplied.

'Yeah!' Madonna agreed quickly. 'Yeah, that's exactly right, Edge. Ben Breslin, he ain't so smart, is what I think. Him and his straight up regular army ways . . . That'd have ended up real bad. Guess that was why he only made it to sergeant and the major got to be an officer in the war, uh?'

'Could be, kid.'

Even when the youngster grinned, his eyes stayed mean. 'The way Cutler handled it, well, we're all kinda like one big happy family again . . . Almost.' He laughed sardonically.

Edge led his unsaddled horse toward the stall the animal had occupied earlier and showed a cold-eyed grin of his own as he answered: 'But not the kind of family that stays together because it prays together, uh?'

Madonna laughed again and agreed: 'That's for sure, brother!'

Breslin's sour-toned raised voice reached into the stable as the sun emerged from behind the isolated cloud: 'All you men! Pay parade'll be at five! Gates'll be opened at sundown so you can go waste what you've earned on them whores!'

'Guess the hope is,' Edge drawled as he began to rub down his horse, 'that it'll have stayed together from getting laid together.'

10

AFTER HE had attended to the needs of his own mount Edge used up a little of what was left of the afternoon by giving Mike Madonna a hand with the rest of the horses. The youngster did a lot of talking, in the manner of somebody who liked to talk but had been denied the opportunity for a long time. Once, when he was in full flood, he interrupted himself to ask of the unresponsive half-breed:

'Hey, Edge, I ain't makin' you mad, am I? Runnin' off at the mouth like this? A lot of the guys here been needled by me talkin' so much. So mostly I don't talk so much.'

'We all get our different moods at different times, kid. I'm hardly ever in a talkative frame of mind. Right now it doesn't matter whether I listen to you or the silence.'

Madonna picked up precisely where he had left off in his catalogue of the crimes and misdeeds he had heard had been committed by certain of the men before they came to *El Alcazar de San Juan*. There had been hold ups at banks and of trains and stages. Claim jumping and rustling. At least two men had deserted from the low paying regular army to join this private force. There had been killings a-plenty by guns for hire, in the commission of other crimes and in the domestic situation.

When the chores were done and Edge stood in the doorway, smoking a cigarette and watching the individual clouds merge into a single blanket, changing hue from white to grey, he cut in on what the youngster was saying: 'I guess when you're not allowed to talk, you do some interested listening?'

'Uh?'

'To pick up all this stuff you're telling me, kid.'

'Well, yeah. That's right. I guess I've always been a good listener, Edge. It's what gives me so much to talk about. Sure as hell ain't too much has happened to me that is interestin' to other folks.'

Madonna bent over a barrel of water to immerse his head, then began to towel his face and hair dry with a horse blanket. But immediately there were sweat beads on his forehead again. Just as droplets of salt moisture clinging to the bristles on the half-breed's face were soon replaced after he drew the back of a hand across each cheek. For with the darkening and the lowering of the clouds that now covered the sky totally, the air had ceased to be searingly dry. Instead it was sultry, maybe threatening a storm: the kind of atmosphere that broke a man out into a sweat if he should even think about doing something strenuous.

'Course,' Madonna went on with a sage look, 'I ain't sayin' that too much of what I told you is the truth. These guys are a long ways from where it's all supposed to have happened. Nobody's had the chance to prove how tough he is so far. Just talk. And a lot of it is maybe that. Just talk.'

'It can get a man killed,' Edge said evenly, scanning the vista beyond the doorway at ground level now. Where there was little activity out in the open. Ed Walsh up on the west wall walkway. Drew Peppard and P.D. Parkin standing gate sentry duty. John Driver and Harry Bean crossing the square toward the barrack after the burial of Stafford's corpse. A man whose name Edge did not know on a ladder at the front of the *vivandero*: with a pot and a brush he was painting out the Mexican term and doubtless would sign-write the American translation in due course. The sutler's store was the final building at the fort to receive this treatment. The half-breed thought only for a moment that it was unlikely Cutler or Breslin had even considered having men climb the slope above the east and south walls to translate the name of the fort imprinted there.

'What's that, Edge?' Madonna asked, perplexed.

'Talk, kid. Some fellers don't like to hear they've been talked about. Especially the kind of fellers who——'

'Hey, you think I don't know that?' the youngster came back quickly, his tone resentful. 'I've been in bad company most all my life, mister. And there was some lessons I didn't even have to work at learnin'. Just picked up natural. So I sure as hell know not to talk outta turn. I wouldn't say nothin' like I been sayin' to you if I didn't for sure know you was one of my own kind.'

'You and me don't have a thing in common, kid,' Edge told him without rancour.

'If you say,' Madonna returned, still insulted. 'So I'm green, maybe. But I ain't dumb.'

'You ever take advice?'

'Depends on who's givin' it.' He had abandoned the urge to anger and was now merely sullen.

'Act a little dumb, kid. Dumb as in mute. That way you could live long enough to ripen out of being so green.'

The half-breed stepped off the threshold, turning to the right to go toward the barrack. And Madonna moved into the doorway and called after him in a growling tone:

'Thanks for nothin'.'

Edge glanced over his shoulder to remind the loose-tongued youngster: 'It's what you know about me, kid. And I'm happy with that.'

The inside of the barrack smelled worse than before now that the weather had changed. Or maybe it was just that the group of men taking their ease on their cots or playing card games at the two tables were dirtied up from the afternoon exertions. And perhaps some of them were sweating in anticipation of the pleasures that awaited them just outside the walls of the fort rather than from the heaviness of the sticky atmosphere trapped inside. Others might well have been oozing the perspiration of fear as they reflected upon the killing of the buck-toothed, ugly Sam Stafford. The first of their number to have fallen before the guns of the Apaches they had hired on to hunt down and slaughter.

And maybe ten dollars a day was not such a good deal when it was seen in relation to the bullet-riddled corpse of the man brought back to the fort draped face down over his saddle.

But for whatever reason the men sweated and stank in the stifling atmsophere of the barrack, they were at least too lethargic or too anxiously preoccupied with some aspect of the past or the future to indulge in very much talk. Of the men who were mostly stripped to the waist or to Longjohns, the majority were sleeping or feigning sleep. At one table two men played cards and three more were playing at the other table. And for the most part as Edge lay on his back on his cot, at first smoking and then with his hat over his face, there were just the occasional string of monosyllables necessary to poker and blackjack to disturb the hot, still silence. For nobody snored and it even seemed that the oppressive heat acted to suppress the deep breathing of the sleeping men.

Then somebody's chiming watch sounded the hour of four and there were some complaining curses as the three men detailed to relieve the wall and gate sentries got fully dressed and reluctantly left the barrack. Edge thought he recognised Jack Maloney's voice call out:

'Any sign of rain?'

One of the men who had just left the barrack answered irritably: 'What's the matter? You're alive and it's pay day! How much friggin' luck you want all at one time?'

'Screw you,' somebody snarled.

Ethan Rankinn growled: 'Keep the friggin' noise down why don't you.'

Then the two card games came to an end. And all the men were sprawled on their cots by the time Walsh and Peppard and Parkin came in. The newcomers said nothing and after they had kicked off their boots and removed some of their clothes they, too, spread their heat-wearied frames on their cots. It then became as quiet as it was ever going to get in a roomful of men who were all either sleeping or had something on their minds.

This faintly uneasy peace lasted until the chiming watch

sounded the third quarter of the hour: and signalled it was just fifteen minutes to the time Ben Breslin had set for the pay parade. When abruptly the fetid barrack was filled with noisy activity as the men rose from their cots and struggled to pull on clothes, the fabric snagging on flesh that felt like it oozed glue rather than sweat.

Edge was among the final group to step out into the murky light of heavily clouded late afternoon. The freckle-faced Pierce Browning was another, and he told the half-breed:

'Never is any need for Ben Breslin to roust us out for this parade.'

'I noticed, feller.'

The squint-eyed John Driver, who had gestured for Edge to leave the barrack ahead of him so he would be last out, added with a sneer: 'Reckon you noticed, also, how some of these guys act like they're scared Cutler'll run out of money before he gets to the end of the line. You know why it's crazy to think that would ever happen, Edge?'

'Because if it happened those who didn't get paid for a week in this place would see to it Cutler paid for not paying them.'

The sneer became a scowl and then Driver shrugged as he muttered: 'What's a smart guy like you doin' in a dump like this?'

'Beside you, a friggin' jackass would be smart, Johnnie,' somebody said in a good humoured manner. Then was quick to add: 'No offence, Edge.'

'Go to hell, George,' Driver retorted without malice as the back markers of the men to leave the barrack aligned themselves behind those who were already paraded in much the same manner as earlier out front of the fort commander's office.

'I been there once and I ain't ever gonna go back no more,' a man with a Deep South accent countered. 'When I was there it was called New York City.'

'Oh yeah, so where are you from, Clyde?' somebody asked.

'Memphis, Tennessee, boy,' was the proud response.

105

'Well, I been to the state of Tennessee a whole lot of times and it was always closed. Never was a Sunday.'

The good natured exchanges were beginning to trigger some unforced laughter from the men as they waited patiently to get paid. And perhaps it was not just the prospect of receiving the money and thoughts of what they could purchase with it which put the majority of the men in a lighthearted mood. Also, the cookhouse chimney was belching a great deal of smoke that smelled mostly of wood, but with an appetizing aroma of roasting meat also detectable.

'Don't you believe him, Clyde,' Ed Walsh said with a gaffaw. 'Ted's lyin' about Tennessee. He ain't never been there. Folks can always tell when Ted tells lies.'

'How so, Ed?'

'His friggin' lips move!'

Walsh laughed louder and it proved to be infectious: perhaps the broad shouldered and narrow waisted man named Ted enjoying the joke against him as much as anybody. But then the door within the porch where Raul Escobar had been executed was wrenched open. And the laughter started to diminish before Jefferson Cutler stepped out over the threshold, closely followed by Breslin who commanded:

'Pay parade . . . attention!'

There was a token scraping of feet across the dusty ground and here and there a back was straightened. But at least this bunch of unwashed and unshaven, slovenly attired men aligned in crooked rows on a military drill square maintained an orderly silence while they were getting their pay. Which was something, Edge saw, that gave both Cutler and Breslin a great deal of satisfaction as they moved back and forth along the lines: much like a genuine officer and non-com inspecting the enlisted men. But they alone were as cleanly and neatly turned out as the humid heat and dusty conditions allowed. And it was only at the faces of the men that the dead eyes of Cutler looked—most times did not need to pause for thought before he spoke a name. When he did need to dredge deep into his memory he would raise his cane and tap its silver handle against his right sideburn. At the naming of each man Breslin, close behind Cutler, would flip quickly through a sheaf of envelopes in a tin box to produce the correct one and hand it over. No word of thanks was ever spoken and the occasional nod of acknowledgement never drew a response from the men dispensing the pay.

Before less than half the men had been given their dues, Edge sensed the tension that gripped the parade. Perhaps so discernible because of how quickly it followed and contrasted with the good humour of minutes before. Then the charade was over, the men allowing Cutler and Breslin the privilege of ending it with much the same semblance of military discipline as it had commenced. At the front of the lines again, Cutler said to Breslin:

'You may dismiss the men, Sergeant.'

And he strode off in the direction of his quarters as the man with the Confederate kepi on his red haired head snapped:

'For them that wants it, grub in thirty minutes! Gates open in an hour! All right, dismiss!'

There was a kind of mass sigh as Breslin swung into an about face and then went at a marching gait back over the threshold under the porch. Slammed the door violently closed after the strange sound of easing tension was followed by the dragging of feet, the rustling of bills and the start of talk.

'Real weird, uh?' the black-bearded Lew Collins said as he shoved his envelope unopened into a hip pocket.

The half-breed had torn open the envelope on which his name was written in a neat style of handwriting that came close to copperplate—seen he had been paid for a full day with two five dollar bills. This as he found himself moving with the crowd back toward the barrack.

'Happens every payday, feller?'

'The same. The one time in a whole week when we all play along with that crazy man's crazy army game. Needles most of us like hell. But we just stand there and don't say nothin' until it's all over.'

'There ain't too much money won't buy.'

'Right, Edge,' the tall and skinny Dale Fish agreed. 'And the closer a man gets to it the more he wants it.'

The limping Drew Peppard growled: 'And if the money man's a crazy man and wants a bunch of tough cookies to act——'

Pierce Browning, his freckled face set with a compassionate frown, broke in: 'I think any man that came home to what the major did after the Injuns hit his place . . . Well, he's just bound to go a little off his head.'

There were some sounds of agreement with this as the stragglers re-entered the barrack. Just as the lamps above the tables were lit against the gloom of evening. Then all thoughts about the tragedy that may have unbalanced Jefferson Cutler were dismissed from the minds of the men who were making financial gain out of it. And the rustling of paper money became one of the dominant sounds again as the pay was counted or recounted.

Edge had returned to the barrack only to get his rifle. And money fever had such a grip on the men that it was only as he neared the door on his way out that his intention to leave was seen. When the blond-haired Ray Wade challenged:

'It'll have to keep burnin' a hole in your pocket awhile longer, pal. Breslin said gates'll be open in an hour. Nobody gets to leave here until then.'

As he spoke he rose from his cot to one side of the doorway and positioned himself so that he blocked the half-breed's way out of the barrack.

'I heard, feller,' Edge said evenly.

Wade showed white teeth and his eyes gleamed almost as brightly as he spread a mocking grin over his angular face. Then he stepped aside and gestured with a hand that Edge was free to go out. Said: 'Just wanted to be sure you understood how things are around here, pal?'

The true meaning of what he meant was not lost on most of the men whose avaricious attention to their money had been replaced by tense interest in what was happening at the doorway. Then the audience was abruptly sweating from more than the humidity of the evening air. This as Edge thumbed back the hammer of the Winchester that was canted to his left shoulder. And said into the silence that came in the wake of the ominous metallic sounds:

'It's good of you to take the trouble, feller.'

Wade's grin had a frozen quality. Then the tension drained quickly out of him as he saw and heard the rifle's hammer eased gently forward. And he said with no sign nor sound of strain: 'You're welcome, pal.'

'Jeeze, Ray,' Ethan Rankinn rasped.

Edge stepped on to the threshold and then paused. Looked back into the barrack with a grin of his own that revealed just a thin line of his teeth and added not a glimmer of warmth to the ice cold glitter in his eyes. Drawled: 'I like to be sure a man's heart is in the right place. So when the times comes, I know exactly where to aim.'

11

SUPPER WAS as good as the midday meal had been as far as Edge's jaded taste buds were concerned. And his appetite for the steak and beans and grits and gravy was not spoiled by the tacit animosity that was thick as the heavy heat in the atmosphere of the dimly lit mess hall. Where he was left to eat in pointed isolation by men who mostly may well have secretly enjoyed the small victory he scored over Wade: but were not about to be seen to align themselves with his stand against the hired gun considered to be the hardest and meanest of a bunch that had no pantywaists. Even Mike Madonna sat apart from Edge, but he had not been in the barrack during the exchange so maybe the kid was still smarting from the put down he had received from the half-breed at the stable.

Edge was untroubled by the cold shoulder. Just as he had been unperturbed earlier by the way in which the sentry on the west wall—named Stuckey and one of the regular army deserters—had talked without ceasing. This after Edge had climbed to the top of the wall by the ladder at the north end to scan the terrain spread out below. Most of which would soon be veiled in near pitch blackness unless the thick clouds broke to let through the moon or a storm swept across the borderland with electric flashes of lightning. The exception was the area where the short spur trail from the fort gateway joined the main trail: where Howie Beach had set up his bordello on wheels. Parked the Conestoga, taken the team from the traces and pitched three pup tents. Lit a couple of kerosene lamps within the hooped cover of the wagon and a cooking fire in a circle of stones between the tailgate and the tents.

It was about the whoremaster and the whores that Stuckey spoke, happy to have some company up on the wall and eager to air his knowledge of Howie Beach who was something of a legend around the army posts and mining camps and other isolated communities scattered over the south western territories.

'Brought a lot of comforts to a lot of lonesome guys, Edge,' the bright-eyed and slack-mouthed army deserter went on. 'Surely was a welcome surprise to me when I first see him come by with that old prairie schooner the first time. More than three years ago, I guess. Made use of the service he supplies a half dozen times since then. And never have gone with the same woman twice. That's one thing Howie is famous for—turns over his stock pretty fast. So it's always fresh when he comes by a place for the second time. What surprises me is that nobody ever set up in competition with Howie.'

Edge could have told Stuckey that at least one other man had been in the same business until not so long ago. Jim Bishop who had operated with a pair of whores named Brenda and Molly from a wagon equally as eye-catching as Beach's Conestoga. But was put out of business the hard way in the west Texas town of Pomona. But the half-breed did not say this, nor make any other response to what had been said to him. And Stuckey gabbed on about the details of his couplings with redheads and blondes and raven-haired beauties that had brought an occasional diversion to the hardship and monotony of serving his country on the Godforsaken frontier.

The man kept up his monologue for something close to fifteen minutes, during which time full night dropped down to envelop everything beyond the reach of the glow from the lamplight and firelight outside the adobe walls of the fort. And it was only then that the talkative man changed his tone and subject to complain, with just mild irritation:

'You ain't been listenin' to a damn word I been sayin', mister. Seems to me you're a whole lot more interested in all that nothin' that's not happenin' out there.' He made a hand gesture to encompass the pitch blackness of the stiflingly hot night. Then mopped at his sweat-beaded face with a kerchief as he allowed dully: 'Not that it matters a damn. Ain't nobody ever paid attention to me much.' Now he grinned and bobbed his head in the direction of the small camp. 'But pretty soon a couple of bucks'll buy me all the attention I need.'

Iron beat on iron and Ben Breslin's Irish voice bellowed: 'All right, friends! Come and get it!'

In the relative quiet that followed the call to eat, Edge warned: 'There were a bunch of Apaches out there earlier, feller. Killed a man.'

Stuckey was affronted. 'You think I ain't been keepin' my eyes peeled, mister? You think I ain't been soldierin' out in Injun country for long enough to know that when an Injun kills a white it whets his appetite for more of the same? So all right, it was just a small party of Apaches you and them others saw out to the south. That many won't start nothin' against this place. But maybe they're waitin' for others to meet up with them. And then, maybe, they'll come at us whoopin' and hollerin'. I'm watchin' for that to happen, mister.'

His bright eyes glared their resentment of Edge and he needed to run the back of a hand over his mouth to wipe away the drool of anger that had spilled while he struggled to keep his voice low.

'No sweat, feller,' Edge answered evenly, and grinned as he used his kerchief to mop his own face dry of salt moisture. 'In a manner of speaking.'

'All right,' Stuckey said, mollified. 'Go eat and don't worry, mister.'

'I'm always concerned when my scalp is on the line,' the half-breed told him as he turned toward the top of the ladder. 'So I'll be obliged if you'd quit thinking about what a couple of bucks will buy you. And start to worry a little about what a whole army of young bucks could do to all of us.'

Thus having alienated another of the ten dollars a day men, Edge climbed down the ladder and crossed the drill square to enter the mess hall and discover just how much of a leper he had become in *El Alcazar de San Juan*. And by accident or design it happened that he remained on the fringe of the activities that occupied the men when they had finished eating. Men who returned to the barrack to strip nearly naked in attempts to get cool. Men who went directly out through the one gate that was now open, headed down the slope to visit with Howie Beach's whores. Men who rode out of the fort, and down on to the north trail that led to Crooked Creek. Other men who took the time to wash up and even to shave before strolling out to buy some female company or riding through the gateway to spend some newly acquired money in town.

The stable was empty when the half-breed went in to saddle up his horse, then ducked his head in the water butt before he led the chestnut gelding outside and mounted. Was aware of being watched closely from two directions as he held his horse to a walk across the square. A man on the threshold of Cutler's quarters—surely the major himself—was barely discernible in the darkness. But Breslin, standing beside the open gate and smoking his pipe, was plainly in sight. He took the pipe from between his near toothless gums and held it up in a gesture to halt the half-breed.

'Sergeant?' Edge said.

'You'll be goin' to town, I'm thinkin', friend?'

'A regulation against it?'

'No. You're the last. Six is as many as are allowed into Crooked Creek tonight. Since Apache activity has been seen in the area of the post. You're the sixth.'

'Fine, Sergeant.'

'Don Stuckey made mention of how you were concerned about the Apaches and the post bein' properly secured against a raid?'

'He talks a lot.'

Breslin nodded. 'About them whores, I'm thinkin'?'

'What he was thinking of, Sergeant.'

'Whores are fine, in the right place.'

113

'And the right place ain't a man's mind when he's posted to sentry duty.'

Breslin sucked in some humid air, missed the lacing of tobacco smoke and replaced the pipe. Spoke around it: 'The major and me have to do the best with what we got, friend. I'm thinkin' that if I passed on an order from the major, you'd be the kind of one-time soldier who'd obey it?'

'Try me, Sergeant.'

'Don't take it upon yourself to ride a one-man scoutin' patrol.'

'Wasn't in my mind, Sergeant.'

'That's good. Once them horny sonsofbitches are through gettin' their rocks off, we'll have plenty of men with their minds free to think about watching for Apaches.'

'And some of them could be worth the ten bucks a day, Sergeant,' Edge responded tonelessly.

The comment and the manner in which he spoke it caused Breslin to direct a fast double-take up at him, ready to be angry. But the man on the ground saw nothing in the impassive face of the one astride the horse to suggest he was being cynical.

'Maybe,' the red headed man with the pipe stem clenched between his gums growled. And remained on the fringe of irritability when he added: 'Keep out of trouble in town, friend. We've got enough bad feelin' toward us there already. And be back inside the gates before reveille. Any man who ain't inside and ain't on official business gets a day's pay docked. Enjoy yourself and . . .' He looked around guiltily and then fleetingly removed the pipe stem so he was able to smack his lips before he murmured softly: 'Have a snort or two for me, uh?'

Edge recalled what the man in the kepi had said about Jefferson Cutler helping him to overcome his addiction to hard liquor. This as he touched the brim of his hat with a forefinger in acknowledgement and heeled his horse out through the gateway. Held the animal to an easy walk on the downslope as Breslin dragged the creaking gate almost closed behind him: leaving a gap just wide enough for the customers of the whores to leave and return to the fort. Then he took out the makings and began to roll a cigarette as he neared the relatively brightly lit area of the camp in the fork of the main and spur trails. Where a knot of men were gathered at the tailgate of the Conestoga, passing over bills to the emaciated old-timer who issued them with slips of paper in return. At the entrance of each pup tent sat a whore—a blonde, a brunette and a redhead, just as Don Stuckey had said. In the flickering firelight they all looked to be less than thirty, not ugly and to have the kind of well-rounded forms which men a long time without female company were expected to prefer: and the simple, crimson coloured and loose fitting robes that draped the women from shoulders to ankles as they knelt in submissive attitudes suggested there was no fakery with carefully placed padding.

'Hey, mister!' the aged and ugly Howie Beach yelled as Edge approached the camp. 'What you wanna ride all the way to Crooked Creek for? When we got much better delights here than anythin' that nowhere tank town ever had?'

The three whores displayed professionally provocative smiles, moved their bodies suggestively within the silken textured robes and beckoned with erotically inviting gestures of their hands. And Edge thought they were very good at this part of what they did.

The hare-lipped Ethan Rankinn was in the group of men waiting for the canvas covered whorehouses to open for business. And the hard-eyed Mike Madonna. Lew Collins with his black beard unusually neat from a recent combing. The big, broad Jack Maloney. Drew Peppard with the gimpy leg. All of these and the rest of the men grouped at the rear of the wagon eager for the action to start.

'The hell with him, Howie!' Rankinn complained. 'Get this friggin' business in business before I shoot my load just lookin' at them beauties!'

There was a chorus of shouting. Some of the men yelled their support of Rankinn and others cast doubts upon the man's sexual prowess in any circumstances. This as Edge rode closer to the whores and directed a short double-take at them: saw just how much their relatively youthful appearance at first glance owed to skilfully used paint and powder. But did not think any the worse of them for this. Everyone had to do the best they could to make a living in their chosen trade—or the trade that circumstances thrust upon them.

'Hey, if you're more in the mood when you get back from that jerkwater town, just stop by!' Howie Beach urged him. 'If we're closed, we'll open up.'

'You won't be friggin' closed!' a man yelled.

'That's if there's anythin' left!' Jack Maloney warned with a gaffaw as he stared at the whores with greedy eyes. 'It could be we'll have worn out what these gals got.'

'Now, now, gents, there's enough for everybody,' Beach assured good humouredly. 'All ready, ladies?'

'Sure, Howie,' the blonde and the brunette responded in unison.

The redhead challenged the half-breed: 'Maybe you're one of them driftin' kind that only loves his horse, big boy?'

Edge struck a match on the jutting butt of his holstered revolver and replied before he touched the flame to the cigarette: 'Well, ma'am, there's one thing for sure. After I take a ride on my horse I always know that whatever's going to ail me can be cured by not sitting down for awhile.'

He had ridden on by the camp and Beach had to call after him:

'Why, sir, it's my contention there ain't too many brides go to their marriage beds cleaner than my girls!'

'Now, come on, Howie!' the redhead countered. 'What do you take these boys for?'

It was Mike Madonna who complained cynically: 'Unless somethin' happens pretty damn quick, two bucks apiece is what!'

'Get to it, gents!' Beach invited hurriedly as some voices were raised, in tones uglier than that used by the kid.

Edge looked back over his shoulder in time to see the whores lower themselves on to their heels, swing over and crawl into the pup tents, swaying their rear ends provocatively. Then the three men with the first numbered tickets dropped down on to all fours and moved in behind them.

Despite himself, in the heat of the night as he rode out of the fringe glow from the fire and lamps and into the stretch of darkness that lay between here and the lights of Crooked Creek, the half-breed experienced a disconcerting stirring of sexual want. It had been a long time since the last time. And in such circumstances a readily available whore could be appealing to a drifting saddletramp with scant opportunity to be selective in the fulfilment of any of his needs. Provided she was something better than an obviously disease-ridden aged crone. But after allowing his mind free rein along this train of thought for a half minute or so, Edge removed the smoke-trailing cigarette from his mouth for long enough to direct a spit at the ground: powering it with a curse. Then had to make a conscious effort to commence his usual habitual surveillance of his surroundings.

This he *needed* to do. For awhile there he had *wanted* a woman. Like the taking of a woman, it had been a long time since the last time he had been required to remind himself of the difference between what a man desired to make life a little easier—and what was necessary to sustain life.

So he kept watch within the restricted limits set by the moonless night for the first sign of an attack by marauding Apaches, a nervous and trigger-happy stranger riding the same lonely trail or—more likely—a man from the fort with a real or imagined grudge against him. But he saw nothing that moved within the radius of his unblinking gaze, and neither did he sense any kind of threat lurking in the potentially dangerous darkness beyond. Eventually rounded a final bend in the trail that followed the course of the dry wash and saw the lights of Crooked Creek and Fort Devlin.

Not for the first time he took the kerchief from around his neck and made it damper than it already was when he mopped the sweat off his face. And not for the first time did he tell himself, a scowl twisting the thin line of his mouth, that the sweat was entirely due to the sultry weather. Had

117

not a thing to do with the strain of remaining alert to possible danger. Certainly was unconnected with any slight difficulty he might have had in trying to keep images of willing women out of his mind.

Knowing that he was trying to fool himself, but reluctant to admit on what score, he spat and cursed again just as he made the turn off the trail and on to the single street of Crooked Creek. But with less force and volume than back at the start of what should have been an untroubled ride: marred by self-imposed uneasiness.

The sheriff of Crooked Creek growled defensively: 'If that's a comment on this town, no-one invited you back, mister. Peaceful and quiet is how we like it here.'

Sterling Schroder was back where he had been when Edge first saw him in the bright sunlight of the morning of this day. Stood on the threshold of the weather-stained shack he shared with Jessica Decker. The woman who stood a head shorter and was some ten years younger was to the side and slightly behind him. Two kerosene lamps burned with a soft light in the front room of the two-roomed shack, illuminating a pleasingly domesticated scene of an open book on the arm of one easy chair and a temporarily abandoned patchwork quilt in the making heaped on the floor in front of another. The woman wore a comfortable-looking, loosely fitted dress that had seen better days and the man did not wear his gunbelt, nor a kerchief: and his hat was hanging somewhere with the gunbelt.

Because of the peace that reigned along the length of the street and into the army post at the far end, the couple taking their late evening ease in the shack would have plainly heard the clop of the gelding's hooves. Got the door open in time to hear the spit and the curse as they saw and recognised the half-breed. The face of the red headed woman, pale and with dark half circles beneath her green-tinted blue eyes, expressed concern for her man and dislike for Edge. Schroder simply looked resigned.

Edge had reined in his mount and now returned his gaze to the length of the street after a glance at the doorway.

Replied evenly: 'It was a personal matter. The gunplay this morning wasn't. Not for me.'

'Lover,' Jessica Decker rasped anxiously. And placed a restraining hand on his arm as she sensed the tension start to build in the skinny-framed man.

'Ray Wade's in town, Edge,' the lawman said and brought a hand up and across to pat that of the woman's on his arm. 'You and he had unfinished business when you left this morning. I'm warning you, same as I've given the word to all of Cutler's hired guns that rode in tonight . . . Any more trouble of the kind there was this morning, you people won't be left to clean up your own mess.'

Edge nodded. 'I'm the last man allowed a pass out of the San Juan fort, Sheriff. So if everyone's been given the word, you and the lady can get back to——'

'Take heed, mister,' Schroder cut in, tone bleak and his world-weary eyes directing an intense gaze out at the mounted man. 'If you people start trouble, it's not just a hick town sheriff you'll have to deal with. I've got Colonel Crispin's backing on this.'

The half-breed heeled his gelding into an easy walk as he acknowledged: 'Got you, Sheriff.' He mopped the sweat off his face with the clammy kerchief. 'But a drink is all I came to town for tonight.'

The sheriff leaned out of the doorway to growl: 'That doesn't exactly give me peace of mind, mister.'

And Edge murmured after an almost imperceptible sigh: 'After a couple I may be able to get a piece off my mind, feller.'

12

MOST OF the splashes of light that illuminated the street came from candles or kerosene lamps behind the unglazed windows of adobe shacks: the shutters left open in faint hope of catching the first stirrings of a cooling breeze that could signal a torrenting downpour·of storm rain.

Tolliver's livery stable down at the far end of the north side was lit by firelight and sounds from within indicated a horse was being shod. The bespectacled man who ran the dry goods store stayed open a few seconds more, until he saw the newcomer to town was not headed for his premises. Then he doused his lamps and locked up his place for the night. Two doors down from the store on the same south side of the street was Edge's destination: the stone and timber building from the roof of which Ethan Rankinn had gunned down Duke Emmet with such a high degree of sadistic pleasure something over twelve hours ago.

In much the same manner as Jefferson Cutler had dictated the sign within *El Alcazar de San Juan* should be repainted to translate the original wording from Mexican into American, so a latter-day owner of Crooked Creek's only watering hole had overpainted *Cantina* with Saloon. But the painter had not troubled to obliterate the earlier lettering and by now the more recent sign had faded to almost the same shade of dingy black as the original.

Four horses were hitched to the rail out front of.the arched and batwinged entrance flanked by two opaque glass windows: such a portal and the clink of glasses and bottles intermingled with the low-toned talk that drifted out through it marking the place for what it was without need of any sign.

Edge looped the gelding's reins to the bleached rail and pushed through the slatted, paint-peeling batwings: and from the way in which there was no interruption in the flow or volume of talk and nobody turned a head or even eyes to look toward the entrance he knew his approach on the saloon had been noted already. And that he had been identified by those who cared about who he was. There was nothing egocentric in the process of arriving at such a conclusion. He had been in enough saloons in enough situations far less potentially dangerous than this one to know that the swinging of creaking batwings always should draw attention toward the new customer.

The place was as ill cared for on the inside as its exterior. The room was just a thirty feet deep by forty feet wide area of hard-packed dirt floor, on which a dozen tables with chairs surrounding them were scattered, in front of a bar counter that ran two thirds of the way along the wall to the right. Light was provided by two lamps hung from the timbered ceiling and six mounted on brackets around three of the walls. None of the wicks were turned high but even in the low level of light it was possible to see how much in need of a repaint were the walls, and just how dilapidated were the furnishings. The sticky air was layered with almost inert tobacco smoke and the place smelled much as the barrack at the fort, laced with the additional aroma of stale liquor.

The current crop of customers adding the latest stinks to those that were doubtless impregnated by time into the fabric of the building and every item of furniture were a mixture of Cutler's men from the fort south of Crooked Creek, uniformed cavalrymen from the army post at the end of the street, and a few of the town's private citizens. About twenty of them in total. No women. All seated at tables in pairs or groups of three and four. There was a game of five card draw poker being played by a quartet of troopers. Everyone else allowed just talk to distract them from enjoyment of liquor or beer. They had been served the drinks by a fat, greasy-haired, unshaven bartender of about fifty. Who eyed his newest patron with the kind of hostile gaze that suggested he would rather see a Rocky Mountain grizzly bear come ambling into his place right then: instead of this glinting-eyed, thin-lipped, powerfully lean, cautiously moving man. On the grounds that there would be a concerted effort by everyone in the place to ensure that a grizzly caused no trouble. Whereas he sensed—or more likely knew from exchanges as Edge was spotted coming down the street—that the issues raised by the entry of the half-breed were more complex.

'What can I get you, mister? the bartender asked, wiping his pudgy, sweat-sticky hands down the front of his leather waist apron as Edge advanced on the far end of the bar. His nervous tenored voice still carried a strong trace of the upper New England region that had been the background to his formative years.

'Beer to lay the dust and a whiskey to slake my thirst,' Edge replied as he reached his chosen position at the bar, where it finished against the rear wall. He had put names to four of the men from the San Juan fort by then.

'Beer ain't what you'd call cold, mister,' the fat man apologised with a lick of his salty top lip as he worked the pump. 'But then ain't anythin' that is on a night like it is, uh?'

'Except for the welcome your local lawman gives to out of town visitors, feller,' Edge answered. And swung around to push his left hip against the front of the bar counter that was crudely constructed of untreated timber, its top polished by usage. Thus was he able to keep watch over most of the room and the doorway without more than a slight movement of his head: his eyes doing most of the to-ing and fro-ing.

'You don't wanna pay too much mind to what Sterling Schroder says when he talks tough, sir,' the bald and crinkled old-timer who had shaved Edge that morning offered. 'Crooked Creek don't have any real need of a sheriff and he does some tough talkin' every now and then just to——'

122

'Didn't used to have need of a sheriff, Fred,' a man as old as Dawkins who shared his table cut in, sour toned. And his weak and watery eyes glared angrily as he swept his gaze at random over the men in the saloon. 'Until hired killers started to walk the street and the army of these United States of America didn't do nothin' about chasin' them back where they came from!'

'Ain't our duty, Mr Pendleton,' one of the card-playing cavalrymen said dully, then added: 'I'll call.'

'Ain't nothin's our duty unless we get ordered,' another growled. And swept a withering gaze around him as he threw in his hand and muttered: 'Fold.'

'Twenty cents, mister,' the bartender announced as he finished filling the shot glass to the brim. 'Unless you want I should leave the bottle?'

Edge was midway through draining the beer glass. Set it down empty and dug for the makings as he instructed: 'Leave the bottle, feller.'

'The major don't like anyone gettin' back to the post drunk, pal,' Ray Wade drawled from where he shared a table with the freckle-faced Pierce Browning and the short and fat P.D. Parkin: all of them drinking beer.

'I don't like getting drunk anyplace, feller,' the half-breed answered.

'Fine, pal. Just a friendly warning.'

'Much obliged.'

'You're welcome, pal.'

It was evident that not just Cutler's men knew there was cause for animosity between the blond-haired and brown-eyed Wade and the dark-haired, blue-eyed Edge. For all other talk had faltered and then been curtailed during the exchange between these two men. And the veener of nonchalance that both men displayed seemed to generate within the fetid saloon a level of tension that naked hostility would not have achieved.

The squat framed, bald headed Ed Walsh seemed to resent the cool self-control of Wade and Edge. He was drinking at a table shared with a cavalry corporal and the man who ran the hardware store. There was a bottle, almost empty of whiskey, standing in the centre of the table. And an empty, perhaps as yet unused glass, in front of an unoccupied fourth chair at the table. This place reserved, Edge had presumed when he first entered the saloon, for Dale Fish who was the missing man of the six who had come to town from *El Alcazar de San Juan*. And with just four horses hitched to the rail before the chestnut gelding joined them, it was likely the tall and skinny man with the scar on his jaw was having his mount shod at the livery that doubled as a blacksmith.

It was Browning who owned the chiming watch. And as it began to sound an hour, Walsh spoke out loudly against the mumbling of restarted conversations.

'Why don't you two guys quit pussyfootin' around each other and settle the score, for frig sake?'

'Ed!' Parkin snapped apprehensively as the talk abruptly subsided again.

'You know the major don't like us to bring our——' Wade started.

The veteran non-com at the table with Walsh broke in: 'Somethin' was sure settled here this mornin' when you and your killin' partner backshot them other two guys!'

'Our business and we took care of it!' Wade snarled, half rising.

Walsh did rise to his less than towering full height. His scowl of anger no longer shared between Wade and Edge as he augmented: 'That's right, bluebelly! And you can butt out of this, too!'

He threw a punch in the direction of his glare. And his fist landed squarely on the nose of the suddenly shocked corporal. Who was tipped over backwards, still on his chair, his arms flailing. Instantly other chairs were sent toppling to the back and sides as a pandemonium of curses and yells filled the room. The vocal din counterpointed by the shattering of bottles and glasses.

The uniformed men were first to get to their feet in the wake of the initial blow being struck. Eight of them, not including the corporal with the bloodied nose, who

124

took much longer to crawl his way up from the floor. Wade, Parkin and Browning were less than a second later in attaining their feet. Then the merchants of the town who were not all as elderly as Pendleton and Fred Dawkins.

Just Cutler's men were armed with holstered handguns. And for a moment there was a move by the local citizens to go for cover while the troopers checked their initial impulse to attack. But then after this almost imperceptible pause it was acknowledged by all the adversaries that the time-honoured unwritten first rule of the bar-room brawl should apply: there would be no holds barred except for gunplay.

And as the fight got started, Edge struck a match on the top of the counter and lit his cigarette: saw the bartender return to its place beneath the countertop a twin barrel shotgun he had started to remove. But the man, the expression on his fleshy and sweat-beaded face displaying little concern about what was happening on his premises, did not move away from where the weapon was stowed.

A stocky trooper thudded a fist into P.D. Parkin's flabby belly and the hurt man screamed and doubled up. But he swung his two hands clenched together in the opposite direction and his cry of pain became a howl of pleasure as he made contact with his attacker's crotch.

Two uniformed figures closed with Wade, who smashed a bottle in half and stabbed the jagged circle of glass shards toward the face of one of them as he kicked the second in the kneecap. The man who leaned back from the threat of a cut open face swept up a chair and whirled. Intent upon swinging it at Wade. But it smashed into the shoulder of Browning. With force enough to send him staggering sideways. Into a roundhouse punch from one trooper and a vicious kick from another. The punch hit the freckled cheek of the man with a sickening sound that was clearly heard above the rest of the din. And the kick cracked into his ankle. He went down hard and a barrage of kicks began to punish him: both troopers drawing back their booted feet to lash them forward into the body and head of the writhing man who soon gave up the struggle to rise.

A man not in uniform tried to jump on Wade's back. But he misjudged the leap. Wade ducked out of the way of a trooper's swinging fist and the man in mid-air took the blow at a closing speed that knocked him senseless. So that he dropped as a dead weight to the floor the instant it connected with the point of his jaw.

During the fleeting opening pause when it was tacitly agreed that no firearms should be used, all but this one civilian citizen of the community had apparently decided that a nine to five majority in favour of the United States cavalry against Cutler's private army was sufficient to win the day over the troublemaking strangers to town. And all save the unconscious man were now backed against the walls and the bar counter. Some of them laughing and yelling in delight. Others throwing pulled punches in imitation of the full-powered ones traded by the men who were slugging it our amid overturned chairs and tossed aside tables on a floor littered with smashed glass.

Two troopers were down and out cold. But the corporal—his face now only one of many that ran with blood—was back on his feet and laying into Ed Walsh with a vengeance that gleamed in his eyes and gave extra power to every punishing punch he launched at the smaller man. Walsh was on his feet, just. And this seemed to be only because each staggering backward step he took brought him up against the support of a table or another fighting man. Once he stumbled over a chair, but managed to drag himself upright again: and not for the first time he attempted in vain to counter the relentless onslaught of punches. But his pathetic defence was easily penetrated by the corporal who was venting gusts of triumphant laughter now: his enjoyment of the victory maybe heightened by the knowledge that he was not a skilled brawler himself. Probably he had never been the winner in a fistfight before. Because he had never gone into a brawl with a man so drunk as Walsh, or one who was even more clumsily ponderous than himself.

Too clumsily ponderous, Edge was thinking when the hollow-cheeked, bulging-eyed Pendleton yelled at him:

'What's the matter with you, mister?' The scorn in his expression was matched by his tone of voice. 'I thought you was one of the Cutler bunch?'

'I am, feller,' the half-breed replied.

A trooper smashed an empty bottle on the back of Parkin's head and the fat man swayed for a moment, on splayed feet rooted to the floor. Then he dropped hard to his knees and tipped forward, rivulets of blood merging with the beads of sweat coursing down his fleshy face.

'A man's supposed to help his buddies in times of trouble!' the old-timer pressed on, his contempt for the calmly smoking half-breed expanding with each word.

'I ain't a man . . .' Edge started. Leaned back as a piece of broken chair sailed over the ducked head of its intended target and spun across the bar counter, taking the half-breed's whiskey bottle with it.

'That surely is true!' Pendleton snarled at him.

'. . . that has any buddies at the best of times,' Edge concluded.

This as the corporal again gave advance notice to Walsh of another punch to the face. And the squat little man—his bald skull the only area of his head not bloodrun—was at his most sluggish as he tried to block the blow. The soldier's fist struck powerfully home and the civilian was forced into another backward stagger. But there were no tables nor chairs in his unseen path now. Nor any blocking bodies of men engaged in different fights. Just two Crooked Creek citizens standing in front of the batwings. And they stepped hurriedly to either side of the threshold. So that the back stepping Ed Walsh smashed into the doors which crashed open and he hurtled out of the saloon.

At the same moment, the bloody-headed P.D. Parkin rose to his feet and felled a trooper with a knee in the crotch and a two-handed fist into the face as the man doubled over. Then was himself taken out of the brawl for good by two more uniformed men who suckered him: one tapped him on the shoulder and as he turned to swing at him the second crowned him with a spittoon. Next upended the spittoon so that its slimy contents were tipped over Parkin's face.

This as Wade went down because of a lapse in concentration: his gaze straying to the batwings that still flapped in the wake of Walsh's exit. Thus was Wade perfectly set up to take the full weight of a roundhouse punch from a trooper much smaller in stature and much less strong than he was. On the way down from the lucky punch he hit the side of his head on a table and was out of the fight.

There was a raucous cheer from the audience. And the troopers still on their feet whirled this way and that, fists clenched and bodies held in attitudes of readiness to meet the challenges of new assailants. But there were no more to be seen. Until Edge seemed about to take a hand in the fight. Took the cigarette from his mouth and finished the whiskey in the shot glass. Drew some coins from a pocket and put them down on the counter top. And said as he repositioned the cigarette and moved away from the bar:

'You mentioned twenty cents for what I've drunk. Somebody else broke the bottle, bartender.'

There was a stretched second of silence in the hot and stinking saloon. Until the corporal demanded to know:

'Just where the frig do you figure you're goin', mister?' His attempt at a harsh and commanding tone was marred by the way he had to press a handkerchief to his bleeding nose, for this made him sound like a man with a heavy head cold.

'Out of here,' the half-breed answered evenly as he picked his way among the felled men.

'Who the hell says?' the small trooper who had finished Ray Wade snarled. And stepped into the path of Edge, clenching his fists at his sides as he spread an expression of invincibility across his bruised and lacerated face.

Edge halted and shook his head very slowly, his features impassive as he issued a soft sigh. Then became still and silent. But a moment later powered out of total inertia. Thrust his arms forward and pushed his hands under the armpits of the little man. Moved his fingers so that the trooper was starting to be shaken by laughter from the tickling sensation. And suddenly exerted force. Lifted his victim by the armpits. To hurl him straight upward. So that the man's head hit a roofbeam with force enough for the crack of hair and skin-covered skull bone to sound sharply. Then the man crashed back to the floor, his legs buckled and he went down into a heap, moaning as he interlocked his hands on his head.

'Who the hell's to say I don't?' the half-breed countered evenly to bring to an end another momentary shocked silence.

Then other men began to speak. And to move forward. But yet again were frozen into mute immobility. This time stunned by Edge's act of drawing the Frontier Colt from his holster. He thumbed back the hammer and aimed the revolver down at the face of the trooper at his feet, the man's pain abruptly displaced by terror.

'Hey, mister, ain't nobody else here packin' a gun!' the non-com complained sullenly.

'The bartender is, Corporal,' Edge disagreed. And a glance of his glinting eyes was sufficient to cause the fat, greasy-haired man to spring back from where he had been reaching under the bar counter. Then the narrow-eyed gaze raked the room as the half-breed added: 'But I ain't fussy. I'll put a bullet into anyone who even looks like he's getting ready to keep me from leaving.'

'At least the other guys played the game and didn't pull no sidearms!' This from a trooper who was holding his belly with one hand and pressing a bunched up kerchief to the side of his head with the other as he surveyed the sprawled forms, some of them starting to move and groan, amid the wreckage of furniture, bottles and glasses.

'Those others will wake up hurting, feller,' Edge answered. 'Me, I've gone that route too often before. These days I like to get what I want without any pain.'

He stepped around the man he had bounced off the ceiling. And tracked the Colt from side to side as he headed for the doorway, covering everyone within his range of

129

vision. Which was enough of a threat to convince those out of his sight that they should hold still. At the threshold of the saloon he slid the revolver back into the holster, easing the hammer gently forward. Paused to look back over his shoulder and add:

'And I gave up playing games when I stopped being a kid. Except for poker.'

'Reckon that's how you got to be so much of a four-flusher,' somebody accused in a sneering tone.

'I wouldn't bet on him bein' any kind of bluffer, Drew,' somebody else put in quickly, nervously.

Edge held back for a moment from pushing out between the batwings. And offered the challenge: 'I drew already. Anybody wants to call, I'll see you . . . later.'

13

EDGE STEPPED out into the night where the air was no cooler than inside the saloon. But it smelled a whole lot better. And maybe the promise of rain was a little stronger now. He thought it was the bartender he heard growl:

'There goes a guy who lays his cards on the table.'

Somebody laughed and it was a thin, nervous sound.

'Sure wasn't nothin' of the four-flusher in his eyes when he looked down at me with that aimed gun in his hand!' This from the trooper who had got lucky with Wade and ran out of good fortune with Edge. His terror was diminishing and the pain in his head now sounded in his voice again.

Then Edge was too far away from the doorway to pick out individual sentiments from the chorus of competing talk that filled the saloon. Had moved out on to the street beyond the hitching rail with the line of five horses standing quietly at it. He halted for a few moments, his back to the arched entrance of the noisy watering hole, swinging his head one way and then the other. Looking for a sign to show which way Ed Walsh had gone after he picked himself up off the ground. Or maybe the man had not even stumbled after he completed his backward plunge out of the saloon, the half-breed reflected as he dropped his cigarette and put a foot on it. Could be Walsh had the strength of purpose that enabled him to summon the willpower to stay upright.

Which was totally immaterial. Just as it was probably of no important concern to Edge to find out why the man had started the fight. Then thrown his end of it. With or without the collusion of the cavalry corporal. Except as a matter of curiosity. Which was not usually a failing of the half-breed.

There were fewer lamps and candles burning in the buildings along the street now. Tolliver's livery stable was still doing late hour blacksmithing business, the hammering of shoes onto hooves ringing out through the part-open doorway which spilled a narrow shaft of light into the night. At the other extreme end of the street, on the opposite side to the stable, a broader wedge of yellow splashed out of the doorway of the shack shared by the lawman and Jessica Decker. There was a shadow thrown by the dim light of the two kerosene lamps by which Schroder had been reading and the woman did her needlework. Somebody was standing just inside the threshold. The distance was too long for Edge to tell if the shadow was that of a man or a woman.

Then one of the few lights that had been glimmering from a window closer to where he stood was now doused— a faint trace of yellow fading into extinction in the alley between the church and Schroder's office, diagonally across the street from the saloon. Edge moved toward the mouth of the alley. His attitude was casual on the surface. But he was tense just beneath the nonchalant veneer. And somebody with reason to direct a second glance at him might have noted that his right hand never swung too far away from the butt of the revolver jutting out of the tied-down holster.

Such an observer was Sterling Schroder. The lawman stepped out of the alley just as Edge reached the church corner of it. And said, a little huskily:

'Smells like a storm in the air.'

'That what it is?' the half-breed answered the man who had buckled on his gunbelt but not bothered with his hat for the walk from his home to his work place. 'I smelled it as the stink of trouble brewing.'

Schroder indicated the saloon with a jerk of his head: 'Awhile back it sounded like trouble had already boiled over in Frank Lacey's place?'

'A few fellers got a little heated, Sheriff. But things have simmered down a little now. In the saloon.'

Schroder's tongue came out to lick some sweat from the bristles of his bushy moustache. Said: 'Fine. And since Frank Lacey didn't yell for me, the law doesn't have to get involved.' He spat some salty sweat-laced saliva out of the side of his mouth. 'Unless somebody——'

'There's a lot of blood, but nobody got killed. Unless a feller named Ed Walsh crawled away to die someplace. And I don't figure he did.'

'You lost me, Edge.'

'And I've lost Ed Walsh, Sheriff.'

There was a brief surge of noise from across the street and both the men at the mouth of the alley glanced toward the arched entrance of the saloon. This as the batwings folded open and a group of uniformed men emerged. Two troopers still pressed bloodied kerchiefs to facial wounds, but only one man needed to be helped by a companion as the group headed along the street in the direction of Fort Devlin. They were several yards away when one of them called in disgruntlement:

'It was a good clean fight, Sheriff! Until that sonofabitch pulled a gun!'

'That what ended the brawl?' Schroder asked, his world-weary eyes meeting the slitted blue gaze of the half-breed. This after both men had glanced away from the departing troopers and at the saloon: knew they were being watched with suspicion from within.

'No, feller. It was already finished. Never took a hand in that fight. And I ain't too happy to be boxing out here with you.'

'You lost me again, Edge.'

The half-breed pursed his lips, then nodded. 'All right. I'll spread out some more cards. There's a rumour that one of Cutler's hired guns is a Government man keeping you in touch with what's happening at the fort in the San Juan valley. Over at the saloon when somebody's watch chimed an hour, Walsh started the fight. And allowed a feller who brawls like a girl to beat all hell out of him. Staged every

133

move of it so he could be punched out through the door. Where he wasn't beat up so bad he couldn't disappear fast. Maybe to have a meeting with somebody while other interested parties were still busy beating hell out of each other.'

'And who else would he meet with but me?' Schroder said. 'Since the rumour has it I'm the one——'

'There were a lot of stinks in the saloon, Sheriff,' Edge cut in. 'And I couldn't be sure if my nose for trouble was confused when the fight set it twitching. But Walsh not being spreadeagled on the street. And you putting in a little night work at the office after I'd seen you and the lady——'

'Has Jefferson Cutler made you his troubleshooter, Edge?' Schroder interrupted, his voice no longer even tenored. 'I thought Ray Wade and Ethan Rankinn took care of that end of his crazy business? The way they took care of it this morning?'

'I last saw Rankinn standing in line to get laid. And Wade got himself knocked out cold because he was watching Walsh instead of what he was doing.'

'So you elected yourself to do what maybe has to be done?' Schroder said. And the tension that had started to sound in his voice was now channelled into a kind of tightly controlled irritability.

'Like I told you, I was following my nose,' Edge reminded. And both he and the lawman glanced instinctively up at the invisible night sky as they felt spots of rain hit their sweat sticky faces. 'When I'm being paid to put my life on the line, I like to know who's paying the fellers fighting alongside me.'

The flurry of raindrops was short-lived. It had ended before the half-breed was through making his point.

'If I say the rumour's wrong and if one of Cutler's men in Crooked Creek tonight is named Walsh I never knew it until you just told me, would——'

'My new boss is against his hired hands making trouble for the local citizens, Sheriff,' Edge broke in. 'So I'll just say thanks for taking the time to talk with me. And you can go on back home to your lady friend.'

'While you go looking for a man your nose tells you could be a government man?'

'Not just me, feller,' Edge replied, and with a just perceptible movement of his head directed Schroder to glance across the street. Where Wade, Parkin and Browning made no effort to be surreptitious in their surveillance of the two men between the church and the sheriff's office. For the three of them stood in the arched entrance of the saloon, the batwings pushed half open.

The lawman licked more sweat out of his moustache and spat it from the side of his mouth. Growled tautly: 'Happy hunting to all of you. But I'd appreciate it if you take him outside of the town limits to slaughter him. Been enough trouble in Crooked Creek for——'

A man rasped from the ink blackness that filled the alley: 'Why, you sneaky bastard, I'm gonna kill you! And to hell with what Cutler thinks about it!'

Schroder had turned and was about to take the first step toward where the shadow in the light showed Jessica Decker still waited in the shack doorway for him. But froze into almost total immobility at the sound of the first word. Moved his head fractionally but sent his eyes to the limit of their sockets as he tried to see the man who spoke the threat.

Edge had draped his right hand over the butt of his Colt as he recognised who was in the alley. The squat, hairless headed Ed Walsh, his voice thickened by high emotion and maybe a fat lip. He said to the lawman: 'It may make the dying easier to know that the feller who kills you is next in line to go down.'

Nothing of what had been said, just now or before Walsh made his presence known, would have carried across the street to the saloon. But the men in the doorway did not fail to see the abrupt heightening of tension that had been revealed by the change of attitudes by Schroder and Edge. They came away from the arched entrance, the batwings swinging behind them. Neither the sheriff nor the half-breed risked looking toward the source of the footfalls thudding on the hard-packed surface of the street. Both

135

of them peering intently into the pitch darkness of the alley, subconsciously willing their eyes to grow quickly accustomed to the near complete absence of light.

'Aw, shit!' Walsh groaned, and then there were sounds of him moving without urgency. But with some degree of effort. 'It matters what the hell Cutler thinks, frig it! Ten bucks a day it matters! And stayin' alive, I guess!'

He started to breathe heavily, wheezing deep down in his throat. Then the three men from the saloon came close enough to the mouth of the alley for their slowly-moving footfalls to mask much of the noise Walsh was making.

'What's the trouble here, pal?' Wade demanded coldly of Edge. He looked meaner, as did even Parkin and Browning, because of the way facial flesh had been misshapen and discoloured in the brawl.

'It's taken care of!' Walsh got in before the half-breed could offer a response. He spoke with breathless effort but there was a definite trace of triumph in his strained voice. 'And I handled it, you guys.'

He stepped out into the fringe of light that reached the alley mouth from the saloon. Not alone. For he had the scar-faced Dean Fish with him—the tall and skinny man draped over his shoulder in that unmistakable state of limp inertia that always signals a corpse. The cause of his death was blatantly apparent: for the wooden handle of a knife protruded from his upper back, left of centre.

Walsh allowed his burden to slide off his shoulder and thud to the ground. And the sound of the impact of dead flesh against the street did not quite mask the utterance— part snarl and part sigh—that was vented by the Crooked Creek lawman. Then Walsh growled bitterly:

'And Schroder was gonna let you guys look for me and kill me because you figured I was the one tellin' friggin' tales! When all the time he knew it was this sonofabitch! And Fish'd be free and safe to go on spyin' and tellin', the bastard!'

He shared an angry glower in unequal parts between the dead man and the sheriff: to ensure that Schroder saw the curse was meant more for him than for Dale Fish.

'I don't know what any of this is about!' the lawman snarled, raking the gaze of his world-weary eyes over the unmarked face of the half-breed and the punished features of the other four men. 'But you better understand this! Get the hell out of Crooked Creek and take your fresh kill with you! And let Cutler and the rest of his vigilantes know this . . . This town is off-limits to the whole bunch of you! As of now! I see Cutler or any of his high-priced guns on the street, he'll lose his freedom! Or his lousy life, if that's the way he wants it!'

Just his tone of voice had betrayed the level of his anger at the start. But then a scowl had started to spread across his deeply lined, heavily moustached features. By the time he was through with the threat, his hands were trembling and it was probably only by a great effort of will he was able to keep the rest of his body still. Then, with a fleeting glance down at the corpse, he started forward. Stepped around Edge and collided shoulders with P.D. Parkin. Headed without a further look to left or right toward the shack at the eastern end of the street. Where the pale complexioned redhead with the greenish blue eyes had advanced a couple of paces. To show herself instead of just her shadow as an added incentive for her man to come home.

'Hey, watch where——' the overweight Parkin began to complain.

'Shut up, P.D.,' Wade cut in coldly. As another flurry of refreshingly cold raindrops was thrown out of the sky. And one of the gates of Fort Devlin was swung shut behind the returned troopers. 'A stagecoach could bounce of all that flab and you wouldn't feel a thing!'

'I sure felt plenty over in the saloon after he started the——'

'P.D., go bring Fish's horse from out of the livery,' Wade ordered, and additionally dismissed the aggrieved fat man by the way he gazed fixedly at Walsh.

'Tolliver'll want payin', won't he?'

The rain began to fall more steadily. The drops not so large, but as cool as before.

'So pay the man and collect later from Walsh. He won't

have to pay to bury the guy he killed, so he can come up for havin' his horse shod?'

Walsh, his expression difficult to read because of the dried blood and discoloured swellings that distorted his face, nodded in response to the implied query. And Parkin moved away to do Wade's bidding, tilting his head back to present his burning flesh to the bathing effect of the rain.

'I didn't like the way Fish was so long down gettin' his horse——'

'Let's go get mounted up,' Wade interrupted. 'And you can tell it on the ride south. Figure I'll be able to give you more attention after the rain had cooled me off some. And I ain't hurtin' so bad from the fight you started.'

They crossed the street, Walsh not needing to be told it was his chore to bring the corpse. At the rail out front of the saloon he elected to drape the dead man over his own horse and lash him to the saddle. The other three swung astride their mounts. The rain continued to fall steadily as little more than a drizzle. But there was a musty heat in the wet air that threatened a storm. Little noise drifted out of the saloon. Schroder or his woman did not close the door of their shack with enough force for the sound of it to reach the front of the saloon. Parkin elected to ride Fish's newly-shod horse from the livery. Told Walsh he owed him four dollars as he switched to his own mount as the little fat man climbed into Fish's saddle.

Then the five live men and one dead body came away from the façade of the saloon and set off toward the intersection of town street with open trail. Far to the south, deep inside Mexico, a sheet of lightning lit that horizon for the blinking of an eye. The roll of thunder came several seconds later, almost so indistinct it could hardly be heard against the thudding of hooves: this noise also a little muted now that the steady rain had begun to soften the ground.

Jessica Decker's shack was in darkness. And Edge knew he was just guessing that Sterling Schroder was peering out at the departing riders. The half-breed elected not to carry this flight of fancy into an assumption of what

138

mood lay in back of the lawman's world-weary watching eyes.

'Okay, wise guy,' Wade announced when they had ridden far enough out on the open trail for the rain to have penetrated their clothing and wet their bodies as thoroughly as their exposed faces. 'Make me feel better about gettin' the shit beat outta me by a bunch of blue-bellies?'

'Sure, Ray!' Walsh blurted, relieved to be asked after the effort of bottling it up inside him for so many minutes. 'Like I started to tell you. It bothered me why Fish didn't just leave his horse with Tolliver and come right back to the saloon. But you and the rest of the guys would have been bothered if I just got up and left the place. And if all of us crowded out of there . . . Well, if there was somethin' funny goin' on, I reckoned one guy lookin' for it on a quiet night stood a better chance of not bein' spotted.'

'Somethin' fishy, Walsh,' Parkin said evenly. Then vented a gust of laughter.

'What?' the bald headed man asked, irritated by the interruption.

'His name was Dale Fish. You said somethin' funny goin' on. I said somethin' fishy!' He giggled.

'Friggin' hell,' Pierce Browning groaned.

'Somethin' funny ain't what you said,' Wade snarled.

'He don't have to,' Walsh muttered. 'A joke is what he is.'

Lightning flashed again in the south. Brighter because it was closer. The thunder came more quickly in its wake and was louder. The rain had been falling for long enough to cool the air through which it dropped. And it was starting to outstay its welcome and become a nuisance.

'Anyway, I got this idea to start a fight. And before I gave it too much time for thought, I started it. And fixed for myself to get punched outta the saloon. Straight away, soon as I could see somethin' else instead of stars, I saw the light in the alley where Schroder has his office. With so much noise in the saloon, I didn't have no trouble gettin' into the alley and up to the law office doorway without them hearin' me. Just got there in time. Schroder was checkin' over what Dale Fish had told him. The way the major killed the Mexican government man. How the bunch of Apaches were spotted and blasted Sam Stafford. And how we're expectin' to get a couple of Gatlin' guns any time now.'

'I never knew that,' Browning said.

'You ain't no dirty spy of a traitor,' Wade growled.

Parkin looked set to say something. Probably to claim that he had picked up the gossip about the Gatlings. But abruptly he realised that such an admission could well needle the already ill-humoured Wade into an even more dangerous state of mind.

'You ain't through yet,' Wade reminded Walsh, with a backward jerk of his thumb to indicate the corpse draped over the saddle of the horse on a lead line.

'Fish was real jittery, Ray. He couldn't wait to get outta the office and over to the saloon. Bawled Schroder out for takin' so long to meet him at the office. Anyway, I had to duck to the end of the alley real fast when they came out. Fish first. And he came my way. Then Schroder. He went the other way. Then Edge showed up and started to talk with the man with the badge. Fish, he stopped and turned. To listen, I guess. Worried he might have been seen duckin' out of the office. But he was worried about the wrong man seein' him. Like you said, Ray: a no good dirty traitor. With that skinny back of his to me. And me no more than a couple of paces behind him. It was just too much. I couldn't resist it. I reckon especially so on account of havin' to let some army guy beat up on me to——'

'Sure, pal,' Wade cut in. 'I figure in your place I'd have done the same thing. Shit, this friggin' rain is startin' to bother me.'

Walsh did a double-take at the blond-haired man. Surprised by the sudden switch of subject that signalled an abrupt loss of interest in the account of the killing. Then, as if to test that Wade was genuinely bored by the incident, the fat man continued:

'Then I got mad as hell when I heard what the sheriff was

140

tellin' Edge here. Tried to swing it around so that I looked like the guy doin' the———'

'Yeah, I can guess,' Wade said. Then eyed Edge with something close to indifference as he asked: 'You didn't like the way the brawl got started?'

'Nor how it ended with him being punched out through the doors, feller,' the half-breed added.

'Edge figured I was pullin' it all so *I* could get to talk with Schroder,' Walsh hurried to put in.

Lightning flashed and Wade began: 'Sounds good. I figure . . .' He broke off as a clap of thunder seemed to shake the ground beneath the group of riders and some of the horses were spooked into nervous moves and sounds. Waited for the animals to calm before he finished: '. . . we got our lumps in a good cause, pal.'

Following this the men rode without further exchanges for much of the rest of the way. Along a trail that was indiscernible in the darkness and the rain, and showed as just another piece of muddy ground in the blue flashes of lightning. But it was no longer a dry wash that paralleled the trail. Rain water from off the high ground of Mexico was starting to flow northward and down out of the San Juan valley, added to by that which teemed out of the borderland sky. So that even when the creek could not be seen between the lightning flashes, it could be heard as a rushing sound of torrenting white water.

For perhaps a full five minutes or so the riders experienced the powerful might of the storm as they moved slowly southward, all this time needing to calm horses which threatened to rear and to bolt as the full intensity of the weather was unleashed out of the invisible sky. Rain that lashed down at an angle into their faces now, driven by a wind that had not made itself felt until the most brilliant of lightning flashes temporarily blinded men and animals and a deafening clap of thunder from immediately overhead announced that the worst to come was here.

For a few moments eyes retained a blurred image of the landscape at night lit more brightly than at noon on the brightest of days. Ears rang with echoes of the thunder that had been louder than a battery of mortars fired close by the heads of men engaged in a massive battle. Skin beneath clothing felt frozen as if by high mountain snow instead of desert country rain. Faces seemed to be stabbed by the needle sharpness of the wind-driven droplets smashing against them.

Then, with a startling suddenness, the centre of the storm had moved northward. But its intensified sights and sounds and discomforts took stretched seconds to subside in the minds of the men before they realised it was simply raining heavily again, the drops acting to cool their punished flesh.

'You know somethin'?' P.D. Parkin said in awhile. And when nobody answered him after a pause that went on too long, he added: 'That was like havin' a lousy toothache. Worth the pain for the luxury of how it feels when the friggin' tooth's been yanked out.'

'You must've been to better friggin' dentists than I ever did,' Pierce Browning growled.

'My old man,' Parkin replied with pride. 'He was a fine dentist back in——'

'Bet it was your wisdom teeth he took out first, pal,' Wade growled. And laughed with genuine enjoyment at his own joke.

'The man said incisively,' Browning added. And laughed, too.

'What's the matter, Walsh?' Parkin blurted, anxious that the good humour should be kept alive. 'Ain't you got any funny——'

'Maybe I'm gettin' too long in the tooth for kid's jokes,' Walsh cut in good naturedly.

'And how about our new boy?' the fat man asked, needing to struggle against an attack of childish giggling.

Edge supplied evenly: 'I guess I can't compete with the biting wit of you fellers.'

There was a spontaneous chortling of laughter that sounded genuine from every throat: far removed from the raucous burst that would have signalled the men were forcing themselves to pretend to share in a mood none of them truly felt. And in the wake of the exchange the new silence between them was easier. Or maybe this had everything to do with the fact that the storm was abating far to the north and the rain was slackening gradually.

Then the night became stickily hot again after the drizzling rain ceased. And a few moments later the group rode into sight of *El Alcazar de San Juan*. Their damp clothing had started to steam toward dryness by then with the heat of their bodies and the higher temperature of the air. But soon, they all knew, the darkly clouded night would be as uncomfortably humid as it had been at the start, and their clothing would begin to be dampened by sweat. Which was one more reason to be grateful that journey's end was in sight.

It was a faint aura of yellow light above the north-facing wall that picked out the fort against the side of the hill on which it was built, the glow thrown off by just a few lamps turned to low wicks within the old fortification given new life.

There was no flickering firelight nor even the faintest glow of a burning lamp in the fork of the trail and the spur where Howie Beach and his whores had sited their camp.

'Damnit, I'm startin' to feel horny as hell,' Parkin muttered as they approached close enough to pick out the shapes of the Conestoga, the pup tents and the hobbled team.

'Beach said he'd open up if anyone wanted him to,' Walsh reminded.

'It ain't anythin' of Howie's that I want to open up for me,' Parkin said. And this time the joke was too weak and the weary mood too far removed from what it had been earlier to trigger even a smile as the fat man giggled. But Parkin did not allow this lack of response to faze him: dug in his spurred heels to send his horse into a gallop over the final fifty yards or so to where the travelling cathouse had come to a temporary rest.

'Hey, mister?' Ed Walsh said tautly after doing a

143

double-take at the half-breed. 'You know somethin' the rest of us don't?'

He had to raise his voice to be heard above the sound of pumping hooves on the muddy trail that was briefly louder than the fast flowing water in the creek. And Wade and Browning detected Walsh's anxiety. Looked hard at Edge in the same manner as the bald headed man.

Browning said: 'I heard from Lew Collins how this guy knew about the Injuns before anyone else on the patrol this after——'

Wade cut in coldly: 'Because he keeps watch everyplace when there ain't nothin' to see. I've been noticin' that. What's wrong, pal?'

Parkin brought his mount to a rearing, slithering, snorting halt between the pup tents and the rear of the wagon. Yelled for Howie Beach to open up his business for a man in dire need. This at the same time as the sentry on the west wall reached its northern end and called down something in a tone that suggested it was obscene. Then both laughed and Edge spoke evenly against the sound to the trio of men at his side:

'Something.'

'What the frig use is——' Walsh began to rasp, anger mixed in with anxiety now.

'You're stupid, pal!' Wade snarled. But was glowering at Walsh when he delivered the insult, as both he and the half-breed reined in their horses.

'Shit,' Walsh said with a gulp as he and Browning brought their mounts to a halt. And also followed the lead of the other two in raking their gazes in every direction. This as they reached for the stocks of the rifles that jutted from forward-hung boots.

They had checked some thirty yards short of the camp. Where P.D. Parkin, still astride his now docile horse had drawn his revolver and was gripping it by the barrel as he hammered the butt on the tailgate of the Contestoga.

A match flared and a lamp was lit within the canvas covered rear of the wagon.

'Sonofa——' Wade gasped.

'What the——' Browning forced out.

'Oh, my God!' Walsh managed to complete.

This as they and Edge jerked their rifles from the boots. Reacting to a different source of light. Needing either to pump the lever actions of the repeaters or merely to thumb back the hammers behind live rounds. But these small metallic scratches were totally masked by the reports of other rifles that reached down from the hill above the fort. The sound of the gunfire lagging far behind the sight of the muzzle flashes that had been seen by the men on the trail. At least half a dozen men, close to the crest of the hill, had loosed the volley of shots. Then they fired a second fusillade. Or maybe these bullets were blasted by other members of the group if they had only single shot weapons instead of repeaters.

The rattle of these firings were not heard by the men astride their halted horses on the trail. And they perhaps did not even hear the sounds of their own rifles as they triggered bullets toward the ridge. For the hail of gunfire from up there had found its intended mark. Which was not the lamp-lit wagon as such, nor any of its occupants or the fat man who was wheeling his horse away from it.

There were sticks of high explosive fixed to the rig. And enough of them were detonated by bullets to commence a chain reaction that lasted no more than a second. And in that fleeting time, to the accompaniment of a roar that shook the ground in the same way as had the loudest of the thunder claps, the Conestoga was blown to smithereens. While in the same moment the ball of fire that ballooned up from the heart of the explosion was blasted outwards. To engulf Parkin and his mount, the wagon team and the three tents.

No sounds of human or animal agony could be heard against the actual roar and its aftermath of echoes in the San Juan valley. Then came the thudding and splashing of chunks of charred and still flaring debris crashing to the rain-sodden ground.

The mounted men instinctively ducked while all their conscious efforts were engaged in trying to calm their horses, which were terrified by the sights and sounds and stinks of the explosion. Each man also instinctively maintained a tight grip on his rifle. Angered by the fact that time was being wasted: even though he knew there was scant chance of hitting a target over such a range on an upward trajectory with only the memory of muzzle flashes to aim at.

Suddenly, in the same way that the full force of the storm centre had pushed northward and left relative peace and quiet in its wakè, so the explosion and the most violent effects of its aftermath had slipped away. There was no more gunfire from the ridge, the shower of fragments of timber and metal and human and horse flesh had finished, the hissing of small fires that still burned over a wide area was masked by the rippling of the creek water, and as horses calmed, their riders ceased to curse. And for stretched seconds this sound of running water was all that kept the eerie silence from being absolute.

Until an uproar of competing voices raised to full pitch sounded from within the fort: and running footfalls hit the square as the men raced for the ladders that gave access to the walkways.

'Just what the frig happened over there?' Ed Walsh gasped from a constricted throat as he stared fixedly in shock at the blackened area of ground where the night camp had been, now dimly lit by the flickering flames of many small fires.

Wade spat the taste of smoke out of his mouth and growled: 'That fat slob Parkin got a different kind of bang from the one he wanted, pal.'

'This ain't no time for makin' no lousy jokes, you asshole!' Walsh snarled.

And Wade simply shrugged, as affected as anyone by what he had seen.

'I don't know about that,' the freckle-faced Pierce Browning muttered absently. As the din from the fort subsided, the men reaching vantage points from where they could look down upon the awesome answers to many of their questions. 'Old P.D. enjoyed a joke.

146

'Even if lousy ones were the only kind he ever cracked himself,' Wade allowed.

Edge was the first of the group to heel his horse forward, after he had pushed his Winchester back in the boot. When a glinting-eyed survey of the hillside above the fort convinced him the sharpshooters had withdrawn. And the others were quick to follow him, like they were each afraid to be left alone out on the trail where he could not be sure the danger had past.

'That's why the poor bastard never had any buddies, maybe?' Browning suggested, just for something to say to help steady his jangling nerves. And he giggled, still in shock. 'Sure wasn't many guys at this place who could stand bein' with him for long when he was tryin' to be funny . . . Holy cow! What the frig's that?'

Edge, Wade and Walsh all swept their gazes in the direction where Browning's shaking hand was pointing. And saw on the bank of the creek in the final flickering light of an almost burned out fire the decapitated head of P.D. Parkin, the gaping wound of the neck where it had been blasted off his shoulder still slowly seeping blood. The face was largely blackened by charring, but the fleshy contours of the features and the open, terror-glazed eyes made this part of the little fat man instantly recognisable.

The half-breed delved for the makings as the four men and a corpse rode on up the sloping spur toward the tentatively opening gates of the fort. Drawled: 'Like when he was alive. The feller ain't got nobody.'

14

THE HUMID atmosphere within *El Alcazar de San Juan* remained charged with near debilitating shock for upwards of an hour after the explosion. And many of those who waited there, most of them kicking their heels, probably secretly wished they were among the six Ben Breslin had detailed to the patrol he led out of the gateway less than ten minutes after the return of the men from town. This patrol, on orders from Jefferson Cutler, was to head up to the ridge above the fort: there to check that the sharp-shooters had gone and then to find out if they had left any sign that identified them.

Not that many, on the patrol or left in the fort, had much doubt about who the raiders were. A bunch who had earlier made a furtive approach to the wagon to fix the dynamite in place. Without being heard by the sleeping Howie Beach and the women or seen by the gate and walkway sentries at the fort. Using the cover of the storm, for sure. But there were times when the electric storm lit up the night more brilliantly than any level of daylight ever could.

Only sneaking Indians could have engineered the slaughter with such deadly cunning, the men were certain. The same bunch of Apache savages who had gunned down Sam Stafford in the afternoon. And thus were the men on the patrol nervously aware that such a silent, unseen enemy might still be up on the ridge: patiently awaiting a fresh opportunity to unleash more carnage on the highly paid hired guns. While the men down in the fort listened in tense expectation for the sounds of a renewed outbreak of violence: and wished they were up there with Breslin, doing something . . . anything except waiting and watching.

While Breslin's patrol was out, the survivors of the round trip to Crooked Creek gave Jefferson Cutler an account of what happened there and its culmination in the knifing of Dale Fish. This in the privacy of the spartanly furnished office of the fort commander. Ed Walsh's version was accepted without query by the grim-faced man who constantly hit the palm of his left hand with the silver handle of the cane as he listened: his mind for the most part obviously elsewhere.

It was Wade who mentioned as an afterthought the threat by Sheriff Sterling Schroder to jail or even kill the major or any of his men who stepped on to the town's single street. To which Cutler replied, with something akin to the light of triumph in his usually dead-looking yellowish-brown eyes:

'If we need to take up that challenge, then we will accept it. But all being well, the waiting is nearly over. I am given to understand that before noon tomorrow we will be fully equipped. And we know we do not have to move far to engage the enemy.'

Walsh's relief at having his account of the killing of Fish accepted so easily by Cutler went some way to calming his nerves, which had been jumping ever since the blast. And he did not feel slighted when he received not a word of praise for his vigilance and the drastic action he had taken. Then he was given the chore of burying his victim and he did it without complaint: welcomed the diversion of some physical labour that helped to keep his mind free of the fears that haunted so many other men.

Pierce Browning occupied his time with retelling to anyone who would listen the details of what happened in Crooked Creek. And many were eager to hear about the saloon brawl and the killing in the alley: if only, like Browning, to take their minds off what had happened more recently and much closer to hand. And what might take place at any tense second.

Then the patrol returned unscathed, the duty sentry and the men who had joined him up on the walkway yelling down the news to those below. And within moments every man except that lone duty sentry was down on the drill square, standing in a loose-knit group facing the open gates. All of them grimly determined to discover what the patrol had learned.

Cutler was on the threshold of his quarters when Breslin and the others rode into the fort. And it was apparent the man wearing the Confederate kepi intended to swing down from his saddle and march toward the cane-toting man in the doorway. But, perceptive to a mood of mass uneasiness in danger of switching fast to anger, Cutler ordered:

'Everyone here has a right to know, Sergeant!'

The gates were closed and secured and all the mounted men save for Ben Breslin came down from their saddles. Then the red headed Irish-American former New York City cop made his report. Did not need to raise his voice too much above the norm since it was utterly silent within the confines of the fort walls: every man eager to assimilate the bald facts that were given.

Ten moccasin-shod men had been on the ridge, having dismounted from their unshod ponies which were left on the other side of the hill. From the expended shellcases it looked like they had been armed with repeater rifles. After they had struck their blow thay had ridden hell for leather down off the ridge on the far side. Headed south. Only when he had delivered these succinct facts did Breslin allow himself to wander into the realm of presumption. Concluded:

'I'm thinkin' the savages are tryin' to show us they hold us in contempt. Rattle us. But what we got to do is——'

The Memphis-born Clyde cut in: 'Well, man, they sure as hell have rattled me. I ain't so sure I wanna hang around here if the stinkin' redskins can get close as they did! And we didn't know a friggin' thing about it until they started blastin'. It could've been——'

'Why, you . . .' Breslin began with a scornful scowl as a murmur of agreement with Clyde rippled through the group of men.

Cutler stepped away from the doorway of his quarters

and snapped: 'I'll order the gates opened in thirty minutes!' This brought silence and he lowered his voice but kept the tone icily cold to add: 'They will remain open for five minutes. Any man who wishes to leave may do so in that period. Without hindrance.' There was another, less insistent stir of rasping talk. Temporarily muted when Cutler warned: 'The men who leave will not, I give you to understand, be in line for the thousand dollar bonus I have it in mind to pay all those who remain! Sergeant?'

'Sir!'

'Come to the office!' He swirled and marched in that direction, swinging the cane in the manner of a swagger stick.

Breslin quickly dismounted and thrust the reins of his mount into the hands of Mike Madonna who had stepped clear of the group. The other men from the patrol ignored the mean-eyed youngster's offer to take care of their animals. Like that they felt that to attend to the chores themselves emphasised that they were not about to accept the invitation to leave. Breslin hurried to catch up with Cutler.

'A thousand bucks,' several men murmured in awed tones as the never formal parade dismissed itself.

'Long dark ride to Crooked Creek, pal,' Wade said pointedly. 'And just maybe the Apaches are coverin' the trail.'

'And what if you make it to town?' Pierce Browning pressed. 'If Schroder spots you, you would wind up dead. He meant it. He was mad as hell at havin' his spy killed.'

'Frig that hick town sheriff,' Clyde growled.

Most of the men remained in pairs or small groups on the square. Edge did not. He elected with a few others to go into the barrack and sprawl out on his back on his cot, listening to the unobtrusive murmuring of distant, indecipherable talk that drifted in through the doorway and windows on the sultry night air.

There was time for him to smoke one cigarette before Breslin's voice was raised: to order the mounting of a six

151

man sentry detail for the walkways. There were to be two changes of this guard during the night, and the half-breed was one of those who drew the early hours relief that covered the period up to and through the dawning of the new day.

A little later, after he had eased off his boots, stripped to his longjohns above the waist and set his hat over his face, Edge again concentrated his drifting mind upon the commanding voice of the Irish-accented red headed man when the order was issued:

'Open the gates! Five minutes! Then secure them again!'

It seemed to be a long five minutes between the sounds of the gates opening and them closing again. Doubtless it was the tension of the silence in the sticky night that acted to stretch time in the imagination. While men waited to see if the man from Memphis or anybody else rode out. And in the backs of their minds considered the nagging worry that the Apaches could spring another surprise attack while the gateway was not secured.

'Close them!' Breslin called, and the relief that sounded in his voice was also discernible as a lifting of what had seemed to be a palpable tension. As those men not assigned to sentry duty crowded into the barrack to flop down in their cots. The Apaches were still lurking out there in the night someplace. And could well launch a pre-emptive attack on the fort before Jefferson Cutler considered himself ready to strike at them. But all the major's high priced army had to do now was wait. Because no man— Clyde nor anyone else—had made the first move to leave, the decision had been arrived at for all of them. And in this respect they were truly an army: a bunch of men either consciously or subconsciously easy in their minds to know that the choosing between alternatives was not a responsibility they had.

'Apaches on the trail worried you some, uh Clyde?' a man taunted softly in the darkened barrack after it had been crowded for perhaps thirty minutes with men who breathed noisily, tossed and turned, smoked cigars or cigarettes but did not snore.

'Up your ass, Ted!' Clyde countered.

Ethan Rankinn said: 'There's things them Apaches can think of to stick up a man's ass——'

'Shut up, old buddy,' Wade muttered.

Later, squint-eyed John Driver murmured: 'A thousand bucks bonus . . . Wow!'

Then, following a pause of several minutes, Harry Bean suggested: 'Hell, that openin' up and closin' of the gate. It was like the line they marked at the Alamo.'

'But we ain't got no Davy Crockett nor Travis, nor any of them kind here,' Mike Madonna said with life-soured toughness.

The black-bearded Lew Collins put in: 'That don't make no never mind. I heard them guys in Texas was up against four thousand of Santa Anna's Mexicans.'

'And how d'you know there ain't four thousand or more of them Apaches out there someplace?' Rankinn wanted to know.

Somebody Edge could not match a name to the voice argued: 'I don't reckon there's that many Apaches in the whole of the Territories and Mexico.'

None of the men chose to get involved in this and a new period of quiet descended in the barrack that smelled of all kinds of bad body odours now that cigarettes and cigars had been crushed out. Again there was no snoring.

'You know what?'

'What?'

'The major was right.'

'About what?'

'Howie Beach. If we hadn't have swung him around to lettin' Howie and the women stay, they wouldn't have been blowed to bits.'

'Nor old P.D. Parkin, neither.'

'Chance everyone took. We knew we didn't come out here on no church picnic. To fight Apaches is what we come here for.'

'Fightin' them bastards is what I'm ready to do,' Pierce Browning broke in on the exchange. 'But first we gotta see them. Up until now they been seein' us first. And if it hadn't

153

been for Howie settin' up his camp out front, maybe them sneaky savages would've figured out somethin' else to show us how they're laughin' their peckers off at us. Somethin' that could've got a lot more than P.D. killed.' He made a sound like a dry retch before he finished: 'Hell, old P.D.'s head was blown right off his shoulders.'

'Goddamnit to hell, it's like the man said!' Wade snarled. 'A chance we're all takin'!'

'Like tossing a coin,' Edge said into the sweat-smelling inside of his hat crown.

'A thousand bucks to the winners!' somebody said, almost joyfully.

Edge drawled: 'And sometimes it's heads you lose.'

15

THE SIX men detailed to the final walkway sentry duty of the uneasy night and the two who stood guard at the firmly secured double gates had the best of the weather in which to be up from their cots and out of the fetid body-stinking barrack.

For the low cloud cover began to thin and disintegrate during the last two hours of darkness. So that even before the grey tinting of the false dawn started to spread across the eastern sky, these men had a clearer view of the terrain around *El Alcazar de San Juan* than any of the sentries who had peered anxiously out over the same vistas earlier in the night.

First starlight escaped from out of a sky that changed from solid black to a streaky mix of many dull hues. And later a low half moon showed itself to serve a useful but decreasingly important purpose, while the end of the night was retreating before the advent of the day.

Then the true dawn came rapidly in the wake of that dull greyness, and there was hardly a puff of cloud left in the sky when its eastern dome began to spread with yellow. Easy on the eye at first, but then growing uncomfortably brighter as the leading arc of the sun inched higher. At the same time the air, which had become pleasantly cool while the low cloud cover was breaking, started to get aridly hot.

During the last of the night and the dawning of the new day nothing was seen to move within the range of vision of the men who stood watch. To the north or south out along the trail that linked Crooked Creek, Territories of the United States with the most northerly community in this area of Sonora, Mexico. Nor did anything larger than an insect scuttle across the drying mud on the slope that formed the western flank of the San Juan valley. Neither was there any living thing, unless microscopic organisms, on the ridge of the hill that curved around the eastern and southern sides of the fort—this the area from which the Apaches had attacked the night camp: which was scrutinised more closely than any other section of the terrain.

Maybe birds were on the wing high in the borderland sky, but no watching eyes bothered to take note of this. For birds didn't bother you unless you bothered them: some of them. Except for buzzards: and they stayed away until you were dead. In the first light of the new day no buzzards were on the ground to feast upon the part-cooked meat of dead men, women and horses that was scattered temptingly on and around the scorched area in the fork between the spur and the main trail. Maybe because, with their mysterious natural instinct for such things, they knew the men on the fort walls were watching for anything that moved. And were keyed up by fear to the point where they would instantly shoot at any moving thing.

The coyotes had maybe responded to the same instinct during the night, when the humid heat had first started on the decomposition process of the dead flesh. They had howled, but only in frustration in the far distance, when they smelled what should have been an easy meal. So maybe the buzzards were circling high overhead in similar states of frustration at the moment when Lew Collins rasped out the warning.

He wanted to bellow the news, but his windpipe seemed to be tied in a tangible knot of tension and the words emerged as a low, harsh whisper: 'Hey, you guys, here they come now!'

Instinctively he pumped the lever action of his Winchester and a live round already in the breach was ejected, replaced by another from the magazine. This as sweat unrelated to the temperature of the early morning air squeezed from the pores of his upper face and trickled into the lush growth of his beard below.

The other walkways sentries hurried to the southern end of the west wall, to join Collins in peering out along the trail from Mexico. A trail that this morning ran alongside a dry wash again, its pebble-strewn bed carrying not a trickle of the night's storm water.

'What's up?' Harry Driver, one of the gate sentries, demanded to know.

'Who's got the friggin' glasses?' Ethan Rankinn snarled after he and all the others at the corner where the two walkways met had failed to see anything but a billowing cloud of dust far to the south.

'It ain't Injuns,' Jack Maloney announced acidly as he lowered the binoculars and fingered his moustache. Held out the glasses for anyone to take them. 'A couple of wagons and some riders. Mexicans by the cut of their threads.'

'I asked you guys . . ?' Driver started, fear and anger in equal measure fixing his tone of voice.

Edge, content with what Maloney had said, returned to the position from which he had watched since climbing up to the walkway—at the northern end of the west wall. And lodged his rifle in the crook of an arm while he delved for the makings and began to roll a cigarette. This as his fellow walkway sentries clamoured for a view through the binoculars, and Maloney waited until some weary-eyed and half-dressed men had emerged from the barrack in response to the noise. Then yelled down to his enlarged audience:

'Collins near crapped his pants when he figured he saw Injuns! I figure someone oughta tell the major his Gatlin' guns are almost here!'

'Keep a look out, you crazy fools!' Ben Breslin bellowed as he strode out of the cookhouse. Jammed his pipe back between his sparsely-teethed gums as he broke into a run across the square. But had no need to go all the way to Cutler's quarters, for the major was already alerted by the noise.

The excitement was dying down as the major, fully dressed and newly washed up and shaved, beckoned for

Breslin to join him in heading for the office of the fort commander. Even though Edge could not see the man's distinguished face when he glanced down at him, he knew Cutler was wearing a smile of pleasurable satisfaction. For there was a lightness in his step the half-breed had never seen before, and he swung the ever-present walking cane with a virtual joyful flourish. Then, when the shorter, more broadly built man came up alongside him he draped an arm across Breslin's shoulders in an uninhibited display of affectionate bonhomie.

The two came to a halt out front of the porch where Raul Escobar had been tortured and executed. And Cutler took a few more moments to finish what needed to be said before he went under the porch and into the building. Then Breslin took a half dozen paces out toward the centre of the square, to turn around and see all the men in the open as he yelled:

'Listen, friends! The major's goin' to be involved in a big money deal with the Mexicans! The major plans to deal fair and square! But I'm thinkin' he's right not to trust the Mexicans to play it that way! So we want every man to be on the look out for trickery from them! But that don't mean you men on the walls stop watchin' for the Apaches! Or the double cross could be worked from outside the walls!'

Breslin fixed the pipe back in his mouth and strode toward the gates. The men out front of the barrack went back inside to dress and arm themselves. One of them paused in the doorway to complain:

'Shit, I guess this means we'll miss another breakfast, Sergeant?'

And Breslin came to an easy halt, removed the pipe and squinted up at the bright sky, his head cocked to one side. Asked rhetorically: 'I'm thinkin' I hear the shade of P.D. Parkin speakin' to me.'

Driver and the other gate sentry laughed, infected by the same brand of good humour that Breslin had caught from Cutler.

The harelipped Rankinn yelled across the square from

the northern end of the east walkway: 'Hey, Edge! don't it bother you some guys ain't about to trust a bunch of Mexicans?'

'My father was a Mexican, feller,' the half-breed called back. 'I'm American, same as you.'

'So?' Rankinn asked sneeringly.

'So Edge wouldn't trust you further than the length of your pecker, friend!' Breslin supplied. 'Keep your eyes open and your mouth shut up there!'

Rankinn sent a stream of saliva forcefully down at the ground outside the fort wall. And muttered bitterly: 'Boy, how I hate to take orders from——'

'Easy, old buddy,' Wade growled as he moved toward his partner from the other end of the same walkway. 'Costin' you nothin' but bad feelin' to do like you're told. But now you got a thousand extra reasons for holdin' on to your temper.'

'Damn right!' Rankinn agreed, nodding emphatically. 'And when this thing is over . . .'

'We'll get to some other business and finish it, old buddy.'

Ethan Rankinn grinned as Ray Wade winked at him and directed a fast glance at Edge on the opposite wall of the fort before he swung around and moved away. And he was still as happy as Cutler and Breslin and the gate sentries when the two flatbed wagons and their escort of six outriders reached the area of blackened ground and made the sharp turn to start up the sloping spur.

Breslin scanned the interior of the fort once more and vented a soft grunt of satisfaction when he saw that only the sentries were in full view. But he also spotted rifle barrels and an occasional hand at windows and doorways and the corners of buildings on three sides of the square. And then most of the men drew back into total concealment as the kepi-wearing redhead turned to order the gates be opened.

They swung apart in time for the wagons and escort not to have to check their progress. And a halt was not called until the two riderless but saddled horses hitched to the back of the rear wagon had cleared the entrance to the fort by far enough for the gates to be closed behind them. By then the front-riding man, who was obviously the leader of the group, had acknowledged Breslin's greeting of a raised hand with a curt nod: and he and all his men had completed narrow-eyed surveys of their surroundings. Maybe a couple of them failed to be aware of just how many pairs of eyes looked back at them. But most had a good idea that they were overwhelmingly out-numbered.

'*Buenos dias, amigos!*' the top man greeted at length, and showed his broad grin to every part of the fort. And the abruptness of his switch from silent mistrust to voluble good cheer drew sounds of surprise from many of Jefferson Cutler's men as the Mexican went on in his thickly accented American: 'Tomas Zalamero is here to keep his *promesa* to *el commandante*. It is important our business, it is done very quickly.'

Zalamero kept the grin firmly in place on his lean, darkly-bristled face as he continued to sweep his gaze about him. Then Breslin approached to become the focus of the Mexican's attention.

'Major's compliments, *señor*,' the stocky red headed man said, and his salute was as sloppy as his pronunciation of the single word in a foreign tongue. 'He's waitin' in his office to see you.'

Zalamero nodded tersely, handed the reins of his horse to the rider nearest him, and then came out of the saddle with a lithe agility that seemed to signal he was not as old as he looked to the sentries up on the walls. Maybe none of the Mexicans were in their forties, Edge thought as he divided his time between the new arrivals and the empty terrain of the San Juan valley that seemed to become more manifestly lifeless as the sun and its heat rose to the point where a shimmering haze began to encroach from the most distant horizons.

'The *inspeccion* of the weapons will wait until I say, *comprender*?' Zalamero commanded of Breslin. He spoke in the same genial tone, and from the half-breed's long-range viewpoint his expression seemed not to have altered from the beaming smile. But Edge guessed that at close quarters Ben Breslin was well able to see through the surface look of the man, and maybe even discern the undertone beneath the spoken voice.

'Whatever you require, *Señor* Zalamero!' Cutler called from the threshold in back of the porch. 'See to it, Sergeant! The crates will remain unopened until an order is given.'

'Sir!' Breslin snapped, came to attention and saluted smartly. Like he felt such elaborately overplayed gestures of respect for Cutler acted to emphasise his disgruntlement with having to treat the Mexican bandit with grudging deference.

The wagons and escorts had travelled a considerable distance: through the night or after an early morning start. This could be seen in the weariness of the team and saddle horses and in the dust-powdered coating of mud that clung to the wheels of the rigs, the legs of the animals and to the clothing of the riders. The men were patently trail-weary, too, as they sat astride their doleful, head-hanging mounts. And it seemed that only mistrust of their surroundings could keep them alert as their leader went to where Jefferson Cutler waited for him. And the stoop-shouldered lethargy of his glowering men acted to stress the spring in the step of the broadly-grinning Zalamero. But, Edge reflected as he took a final pull against his cigarette and then arced the butt out over the wall, among the many considerations a bone-weary man might think about to keep exhaustion at bay was the prospect of high reward. And maybe Tomas Zalamero knew just how much Jefferson Cutler was going to pay for the Gatling guns: certainly as the leader of the bandits, he would claim the lion's share of the take.

Then, after a brief handshake on the threshold, the two men went out of sight into the office of the fort commander, and the door closed behind them. It was not forcefully slammed, but the sound of the door coming into contact with the frame rang out with a quality that in the present situation acted in the surrounding silence to punctuate the tension. It neither eased nor built it. Simply held every-thing and everybody in a kind of suspended animation set

161

to endure until the private bargaining of the gun purchase deal had been completed.

In the way that a group of more or less uniformly attired Indians are virtually indistinguishable one from another in the eyes of white men who have reason to fear them, so the Mexicans seemed to be much of a muchness as they waited for their leader to finish his business with the leader of the Americans. And in hindsight, apart from his buoyant demeanour, Tomas Zalamero could be recalled as lacking in any conspicuous individuality. Thin men, all of them: some taller than others, but none extraordinarily so. Underfed but not emaciated. Garbed in pants, shirts, boots and sombreros. Some of the hats were of straw, some of felt. Three men wore ponchoes. A couple of the horsemen had rifles in forward-hung boots. Most, like the drivers of the wagons, carried their repeaters slung across their backs. Some wore crossed bandoliers. All had gunbelts slung around their waists, the butts of Colt revolvers jutting from the holsters.

The men looked older than they probably were not just because of trail weariness. Also they were bearded with at least three days' growth of bristles. And the underfed hollowness of their faces, only partially visible in the morning shade of their sombrero brims, also added unlived years to their appearance.

Without exception the men's clothing was ragged and filthy. But, as befitted bandits in the business of gun running, their rifles and sidearms looked to be almost new.

Their horses and saddles and bedrolls all seemed to be as worn out from ill use and neglect as the clothing of the men. Which placed Zalamero and his bunch low down in the estimation of Edge at first impression. With no chance of getting a higher rating. Men, no matter which side of the law they were on, deserved no respect if they did not take the trouble to care for their horses. And the rest of their gear: not just their guns.

Minutes began to be stretched in the minds of the men who waited. The chiming pocket watch—the half-breed recalled it was carried by Pierce Browning—sounded eight times in the stable. Some flies that had gorged themselves on the torn-apart remains scattered in the area of the former night camp now began to enter the fort and bother living things. And horses flicked their tails and tossed their heads. While men batted or slapped their hands. These gestures of irritation were the only movements made. And the occasional crack of a bare hand on a bare arm, sometimes accompanied by a low voice curse, were the only sounds.

Until Tomas Zalamero flung open the door in the porch and strode out into the sunlight ahead of Jefferson Cutler, who emerged from the office with a less flamboyant gait. But the American looked to be perfectly well satisfied with the deal that made the Mexican so exuberantly happy.

'*Bueno!*' Zalamero yelled delightedly, holding aside his poncho so that he could pat a bulging pocket of his shirt that was obviously stuffed with newly acquired bills. '*Mucho bastante, amigos!*'

There was a visible lightening of the spirits of the bandits. One of the wagon drivers asked for permission to get astride his horse, and when this was given by Zalamero both men climbed down hurriedly from their seats and headed for the animals hitched to the back of the rear wagon.

'We gonna get to see what they've bought, Major?' Breslin asked, and the way in which he stepped between Zalamero and his horse abruptly checked the easing of tension.

'Do that, Sergeant,' Cutler agreed, having come to a halt midway between the office doorway and the wagons. Began hitting a palm with the handle of his cane.

The bandit chief came to a more abrupt stop. And looked to be on the point of explosive anger. His men and the Americans on the walls and in cover were held rigidly on the verge of violent action while Tomas Zalamero struggled against the impulse to rage. Then pent-up breath was exhaled from many mouths as the Mexican nodded vigorously, threw his arms out to the sides in a gesture of easy submission and announced:

'*Si!* Yes! Okay! Of course, it is right to do this!'

Breslin allowed himself a brief smile of triumph directed exclusively at Tomas Zalamero, then swung around and climbed up on to the rear of the first wagon. Like the one from which the former drivers were untying their horses, it was loaded with one large wooden crate and several smaller ones.

'*El pie de cabra, sargento* . . . it is on the other side,' the bandit leader said as he took the reins of his horse and swung up into the saddle. '*Creo que si.*'

'Shit, I ain't got nothin' to——' Breslin growled.

'He says there's a crowbar on the other side, feller!' Edge called down.

'Thanks!' Breslin responded, and pointedly looked toward the half-breed to distance Zalamero from the terse expression of gratitude.

'No sweat.'

The Irish-American located the tool and began to use it on the largest crate that was some seven feet long by four wide and high. And as he worked at dismantling the top from the sides and ends, Zalamero signalled for his men to gather their horses close to his. Then, when their leader lit a cheroot, some of the others felt free to smoke, too. Also, they took their mood from him once more. All of them seeming to be faintly amused by the way in which Ben Breslin worked so eagerly at his chore.

Although there were no markings on the crates, they were obviously assembled in a factory. Inside the larger one there was a great deal of strawlike packaging material, which Breslin clawed away to reveal a Gatling gun mounted on a wheeled carriage. It was brand new and gleaming. The frame and carriage were painted green, the barrels were polished gun metal and the top of the magazine was burnished brass.

'Okay?' Zalmero asked in the manner of a man who was confident all was fine.

'Still checkin', Major,' Breslin said quickly. And removed the magazine cover to check there was no danger before he turned the operating crank.

164

Zalamero shrugged and executed the raised arms movement again.

Breslin nodded his satisfaction after he had listened for a few moments to the well-greased smoothness of the Gatling's mechanism. Announced: 'Now for the ammunition, Major.'

'Go ahead, Sergeant,' Cutler replied.

Zalamero growled: '*Caca de toro!*'

Breslin levered the top off one of the three feet by two feet by one foot crates and called: 'What'd he say then, friend?'

Edge supplied: 'Bullshit, feller.'

'All the best armies run on it, *amigo*,' Breslin said to Zalamero as he revealed that the crate contained a closely packed consignment of brass-jacketed cartridges. 'Forty-five calibre, just like the gun takes,' he announced, straightening up and taking out the big Colt he carried in his tied down holster.

Again, Zalamero's confident attitude made it certain that he had delivered the goods as ordered. The shell taken from the crate and inserted into a chamber of Breslin's Colt to replace the one he extracted fired with the expected crack into the bright sky above the fort. Some horses whinnied at the suddenness of the violent sound. And Zalamero, his tone now irritable with impatience, insisted:

'*Madre de Dios*! You think we would try to cheat you? When we are so few and you are so many?' This time he raised just one hand, to brandish it in a sweeping motion that indicated he knew he and his group were being watched by armed men from all sides. 'We are leaving now, *el commandante!* I *requerir* you open the gates. If all is well on the first wagon, on the second wagon, also. I think?'

'Certainly, *Señor* Zalamero,' Cutler agreed readily. 'Have the sentries open the gates, Sergeant!'

'Sir!' Breslin snapped the acknowledgement as he leapt down from one wagon and started toward the second, swinging the crowbar in much the same way as Cutler was wont to swing his cane. 'You heard the Major's command!' he rasped at the two men who flanked the gates. Then added as he climbed up aboard the other wagon: 'I'm thinkin' that unless they head out hell for leather they'll still be in range by the time I've checked this load.'

Zalamero glowered as he clucked his horse into slow movement, and when he was out front of his men, they started their mounts. All of them were mistrustful again, scowling suspiciously to left and right as their leader said harshly:

'*Señor* Jefferson Cutler gave me his word we would be allowed to leave without——'

'And it was given in good faith!' Cutler countered, checking his intention to half turn and head for his quarters as the gates were dragged wide.

'You're the only one that did, pal!' Ray Wade yelled from the top of the wall at the south east corner of the fort. And snapped his Winchester to the aim. Added: 'Ethan, old buddy!'

It was apparent that the two of them had made prior plans for the move. Because the harelipped man at the other end of the east wall walkway showed no sign of surprise and he did not hesitate a moment before he aped Wade's actions: angled his rifle down at where the eight Mexican bandits had abruptly reined in their mounts.

Some of the riders spat out their cheroots, cursing. Others tore them from between their lips to hurl them viciously at the ground. Where they lay in the dust, smoke rising from them, reminding some of the watchers of the aftermath of last night's explosion.

'I'm with you two guys!' Clyde from Memphis yelled. And stepped into sight at the barrack doorway.

'Count me in!' the rangy man named Stuckey added in high excitement as he emerged to stand beside Clyde.

The both of these had their rifles levelled from the hip while Wade and Rankinn drew beads from their shoulders.

'Butt out, bastards!' Rankinn roared in a rage. 'Me and Ray figured it first! And we're not gonna share——'

'Shut up, old buddy!' Wade snapped, and suddenly sounded anxious.

'The hell I will!' Rankinn argued. 'Cutler . . . Mr Cutler, sir! Want you to remember who thought this up when it comes to divvying the money you was gonna pay for them Gatlin' guns . . . Sir!'

There was a ripple of nervous talk among the bandits. Which was abruptly curtailed when Zalamero snarled:

'*Callarse!*' He wrenched his head from side to side and up and down: checking to see if there were any other men overtly aiming threatening guns at him and his group. Finally he glared fixedly at Jefferson Cutler to accuse: 'You are one double crossing *hija de puta!* And I think——'

'Just give the word, Major!' Wade yelled. And his anxiety had receded or been brought under tighter control as the tall, grey-haired man with the cane remained in the half-turned attitude, his face averted from the four men who were covering the Mexicans.

One of the few who could see Cutler's face was Edge. And the half-breed saw the rapid changes of expression that came and went across the distinguished features. First incredulity. Then fury. Next a kind of pathetic helplessness. Finally a desperate plea for assistance that glintingly enlivened his dead eyes as he announced, unhurriedly, in a faintly tremulous voice:

'I gave my word.'

'So friggin' what?' Rankinn snarled.

Cutler screwed his eyes tightly shut as Rankinn spoke, like he was concentrating against the danger of losing the thread of what he was saying before the interruption. Then he was dead-eyed again as he offered: 'A double bonus to every man who assists in quelling the mutiny.'

There was a tense silence that lasted no longer than a second after Cutler finished speaking. Then a gunshot and its effect acted to make up the minds of the undecided slow thinkers. It was Edge who triggered the shot, the instant the stock of the Winchester was pressed to his shoulder. And the bullet cracked from corner to corner of the fort. To tunnel into the chest of Ray Wade. The impact sent the blond haired man staggering back against the wall. From which he bounced forward. There was blood staining his shirt by then. And the realisation of imminent death showed on his face. The rifle slipped from his trembling hands and

167

he fell hard on to his knees. Teetered on the lip of the walkway for as long as it took the discarded Winchester to clatter to the ground. Then he died and followed the weapon, dropping from sight behind the stable.

The sound of his limp, lifeless body hitting the hard-packed dirt was masked by the pandemonium that abruptly broke out. Of roaring voices and crackling gunfire. That remained at a deafening peak for perhaps five seconds. In which time Clyde and Stuckey were put to brutal death under a barrage of shots. From within the barrack at first, the thudding of bullets into their backs acting to pitch them to the ground several feet distant from the doorway. And then their blood-gouting corpses were riddled with shots from longer range. So for a few moments the lifeless men were made to twitch and jerk, like string puppets, as the lead tore into their dead flesh. This not an obscenely futile gesture by blood-lusting sadists. Instead it was performed out of avarice by professional gunmen determined to share in the promised higher pay-off.

Black powder-smoke drifted and began to disintegrate in the bright morning air. The body of sound comprised of so many raucous voices started to lose its intensity. Men who had previously been in cover now stepped out into the open. And none aimed his rifle or revolver at the group of mounted Mexicans who had made no move to draw their weapons. All eyes swept their gazes toward the northern end of the east wall of *El Alcazar de San Juan*. And then, a few moments later, there were just two sounds audible within the fort. The droning of flies gorging on the freshly-spilled blood of the three new corpses. And the whimpering of Ethan Rankinn as the man knelt at the top of the wall, his arms thrust high in the air to emphasise that his splayed hands were empty.

'It was Ray's idea!' he sobbed, his eyes streaming tears down his bristled cheeks. 'You guys know how he always made me do like he told me!'

Edge canted his rifle to his shoulder now that his part in the brutal episode was done. He had killed Wade and then tracked the Winchester to cover Rankinn. Which had been enough to have the harelipped man toss aside his repeater and drop to his knees as his hands clawed at the sky.

'Why, you snivellin' excuse for a man!' Ben Breslin accused the weeping, pleading Rankinn. And again drew the big Colt from his holster.

'Hold it, Sergeant,' Cutler said as Breslin aimed the revolver at arm's length and the quaking Rankinn struggled to his feet without bringing his arms down.

'Sir!'

'Rankinn, come on down here!'

'Yeah! Sure, Major! Anythin'! You just say the word!' Rankinn kept up a constant stream of talk that promised agreement with all that would be required of him as he scrambled down the ladder. Was out of sight behind the cookhouse for a few moments, but remained audible.

Anticipation had a near palpable presence as the fast-talking man came across the square and then swung wide to go around the wagons and the mounted Mexicans: intent upon getting to Jefferson Cutler. By now every firearm except for Breslin's Colt had been replaced in its holster or was held in an easy, unaggressive attitude.

'That's far enough,' the man hitting his palm with the silver handle of the cane instructed as Rankinn reached a point midway between him and the Mexicans.

Rankinn shuffled to a halt and broke off in mid-sentence. Looked around him and only now realised his compliance and his pleas had gained him nothing. Then he snapped his head around to look back at Cutler as the man with the power of money at his command said:

'*Señor* Zalamero?'

'*Si, el commandante?*'

'I feel honour bound to offer you the life of this apology for a ——'

'No!' Rankinn shrieked. And fell to his knees again. Then went down on to all fours and began to crawl toward Cutler. 'Please! No! I'll do anythin'! It wasn't my fault . . .'

Body-shaking sobs made what he was saying incomprehensible. He left a trail of water on the dusty ground behind him as he lost control of his natural functions.

Zalamero nodded and said to Cutler: '*Se lo agradezco, el commandante.*' Then he spoke in lower tones to the men who flanked him.

These two were as agile as their leader had been in leaving their saddles. One removed the lariat from where it was draped over the horn and the other went to claim the prisoner: got a grip on him just as Rankinn's outstretched hands were clawing at the polished boots of Jefferson Cutler. The mind-paralysing effect of the hapless man's terror was seen in the way he was suddenly drained of the physical capability to resist. First when his revolver was slid out of the holster and tossed aside. Then as he was hauled by the ankles away from the tall figure of Cutler. He could only cry like a defeated child and clench and unclench his fists as a length of rope was tied around his ankles: the other end made fast to the horn of Tomas Zalamero's saddle.

The two men remounted and the leader of the group nodded in final acknowledgement to Cutler. Then the Mexicans moved slowly out of the fort. And Ethan Rankinn forced himself over on to his back as he was dragged through the gateway. Began to shriek obscenities as a mixture of rage and terror displaced self-pity.

Then, as Ben Breslin went to work with the crowbar on the crates aboard the second wagon, Cutler ordered the gates secured, the dead removed to the burial ground and the team horses attended to. And men had started to comply with these edicts before the cane-swinging Cutler completed striding to his quarters. They jumped to obey in the manner of serving soldiers carrying out the orders of a regular officer on a genuine military post. Maybe eager to be occupied so that their consciences had little opportunity to trouble them over their parts in the shooting down of men who had been their partners. Or perhaps, Edge reflected wryly as he glanced at the hive of activity within the walls, they were stimulated to greater efforts because of the way Jefferson Cutler had started to offer thousand dollar bonuses at the drop of a hat.

After this, the half-breed returned his full attention to the sun-baked terrain beyond the walls of the fort. And paid only scant attention to the group of riders who continued to maintain a slow pace down the slope of the spur. He could just make out, against the clopping of hooves, the less forceful shrieking of Ethan Rankinn as the doomed man pleaded with or cursed his captors. Then, after making the turn to the south around the blast and fire charred campsite, Zalamero spurred his horse into a gallop. His men were just a moment later in asking the same speed of their mounts. And the thundering of pumping hooves totally drowned out any sound that came from the throat of the viciously punished man who was dragged at high speed along the abrasive surface of the rock-hard trail.

Within a few seconds a cloud of grey dust raised by Zalamero's horse totally enveloped the helpless man on the end of the rope. And then more dust exploded from beneath the galloping horses behind settled, and served to dull the vividness of the crimson stain that began to be laid along the centre of the trail.

Lew Collins moved from one end of the east wall to the other, and grimaced as he growled against the diminishing sounds of the thundering hooves: 'Sonofabitch, Edge! That's a lousy way to go.'

The half-breed delved for the makings as he answered: 'There ain't too many good ways.'

Out on the south trail, a single gunshot cracked out. And a second or so later the group of men riding behind Zalamero briefly split into two. Then formed up again. And as the distance widened and the dust settled, a humped form could be seen on the trail: totally inert.

'They shot him and cut him loose!' the black bearded man yelled down into the fort. Then, after the news had drawn no noticeable reaction from below, Collins sighed and said to Edge: 'I reckon Rankinn didn't mind so much gettin' shot. Been ready to die.'

The half-breed nodded and drawled: 'Guess so, feller. Way life had gotten to be such a drag.'

16

AFTER TOMAS Zalamero and his men had ridden into the shimmering heat-haze that veiled the southern section of the San Juan valley, before the trail swung out of sight of Edge and Collins on the west wall, the panoramic vistas over which the sentries raked their watchful gazes were again without visible life. Only the mirages of the vapour-like heat seemed to move, and these ghostly motions acted to invest the corpse of Ethan Rankinn and the scattered remains of the longer dead closer to the fort with an utter stillness of greater intensity.

Within the walls of *El Alcazar de San Juan*, Jefferson Cutler had remained in his quarters after engaging in a brief conference with Ben Breslin. As a result of the exchanges between these two, Breslin had emerged with a string of orders that gave every man a duty to perform. That these details were undertaken with less enthusiasm than immediately in the wake of the early morning violence probably had less to do with troubled consciences than with the rising heat of the day.

The strength of the wall sentries, reduced to four by the killings of Wade and Rankinn, was made up to six. And although it was past time when the original guard should have been relieved, none of them complained to each other or to the red headed Irish-American. For although it was hotter up on the unshaded wall walkways than a lot of other places in the fort, there was no manual labour involved in the sentry duty. The work being done in the stables, the cookhouse, the magazine and on the

172

Gatling-carrying wagons was much harder and more uncomfortable.

But if anybody engaged in any duty felt moved to gripe, he spoke in low tones. And probably told himself it was too damn hot to get excited about any damn thing. Maybe the less perceptive genuinely thought this was all. But those with a mysterious sense for such things detected trouble in the hot, bright, almost rasping arid air. They smelt it drifting past their nostrils: less pungent than the gunsmoke of the recent violence, maybe, but strong enough to make itself known to those who had experience of it before. An insubstantial, indefinable sign that the killing dawn was the prelude to a murderous day.

Or was it . . ? Edge was one of those who heard the jangling of silent warning bells from the deep blackness at the back of his mind. And he was up on the north end of the west wall walkway. Above the claustrophobic confines of all four walls and able to see out over the parched wilderness from where an attack would be launched against *El Alcazar de San Juan*. And so if the Apaches were to come, he would be among the first to see the war-painted, whooping and hollering Indian braves. But the valley and its trail alongside the dry wash remained silent and empty for one long minute after another. Likewise nothing and nobody showed on the skylines of the flanking hills—to the west, or the north and east from which the long-range assault on the travelling whorehouse was launched in the night.

Edge did not consider that he possessed an imagination. Perhaps way back in the dim and distant past of his childhood on an Iowa farmstead he had been equipped with such. But there had been too much of the harsher side of reality filling his life since those days had come to an end. A time during which the temptation of indulging in the luxury of imagination was an invitation to be afraid of every shadow and to react violently to every shadow that moved.

Today, out amid the wilderness of this brutal borderland, there were no shadows of which to be suspicious. For the only ones that moved beyond the adobe walls of the fortress were of inanimate natural features on the scorched landscape: pushed around in a slow, distorted arc by the age-old progress of the sun across the southern dome of the sky. But such was the quality of expectation permeating the atmosphere, even a man such as the half-breed needed often to blink the glittering slits of his ice-blue eyes: and then to do double-takes at the ridges or the heat shimmer. To persuade himself that he was simply imagining hostile watchers.

Then came the mundane call to breakfast. And those men who sensed impending violence were convinced they should pay even greater attention to their instincts. For they became aware of the strong aromas of coffee and fried bacon and chili beans that had started to reach every corner of the fort since shortly after the cookhouse fires were rekindled. The stink of future death had insinuated itself through these actual fragrances. And it remained as a constituent of the air while the men ate.

But few were affected to the extent that they failed to scrape their plates clean of what was provided: most eating in the mess, but some using the excuse of bringing food to the sentries to come up onto the walls. In the chain of command that had been established within the vigilante army, only Jefferson Cutler or Ben Breslin was likely to object to this or any other aspect of how the fort was operating. But neither the man who liked to be called by his old rank nor the one who wore the Rebel kepi and the sergeant's chevrons chose to take exception to what was taking place. For all their orders had been carried out.

The Gatlings had been secured to the wagons, fresh horses had been prepared to put into the traces and drivers and two-men teams to fire the guns had been detailed. Every mount was ready for riding, save only for the cinching of a saddle to his back. New rifles and sidearms and an adequate supply of ammunition had been issued to every man who required it. A fully-supplied chuck wagon awaited only a team. And there was even an ambulance parked alongside the chuck wagon, in back of the Gatling-carrying rigs, out front of the quartermaster's store.

Thus, as the men lingered over refilled coffee mugs after they had eaten the late breakfast, those who had served their time in the army proper were able to reflect that this bunch was not too far removed in yet another respect. It was all hurry up and wait. And as each sluggish minute followed another, this waiting drew more and more unwashed, unshaven, mostly partially clothed men up the ladders to the wall walkways. Where, like the designated sentries, they were in a position to see what was going to hit them before the first shot was fired.

'You know somethin'?' Lew Collins said as the sun inched close to its mid-morning spot in the cloudless sky. This as he handed the binoculars into the eager hands of Mike Madonna after he had raked the horizons with the glasses from the south, across the west and to the north.

'It's the waiting that gets you, feller?' Edge suggested as he struck a match and lit what he thought was his third cigarette more than usual for this time of the day.

'That's for sure,' the black bearded man allowed, glancing along the line of grim faced men on the west wall. 'But what I was goin' to say is that Cutler's plans have changed, seems to me. I reckon we was gonna go out lookin' for the Injuns at the start. But now we're gonna wait for them to come to us.'

With so many pairs of anxious eyes scanning the landscape for the first sign of an attack, Edge felt able to relax his vigilance without any qualms. And not for the first time did he turn his attention away from the heat-hazed horizons to north and south and the dazzlingly bright skyline across the valley. But whereas before he had taken the time to surreptitiously glance toward Ed Walsh, who seemed to be more intent than anyone else in the search for movement on a dead piece of country, now he raked his glinting-eyed gaze over the drill square and its surrounding buildings.

Where he saw Ben Breslin beside the cookhouse doorway: seated in rocking chair, alternately sipping at a mug of coffee and sucking on his pipe. Over such a distance the half-breed was unable to see the expression on the red face of the red headed man, but there was about his posture in the chair and the slow way in which he rocked himself the look of contentment. And doubtless he was easy in his mind. For he was a mere sergeant who had seen that the orders of his commanding officer were carried out to the best of his ability. He had not originated the orders and so, whatever the outcome, no responsibility would attach to him. Of course, since he could not be blamed for failure, neither was he in line for praise in the event of success. Which was all right for the likes of Ben Breslin. Army sergeants were invariably so inclined.

Jefferson Cutler was not in such a composed frame of mind as he stood between the posts that supported the porch at the front of the fort commander's office. As with Breslin, Edge could not see the man's features and the expression that formed them between the long, grey sideburns. But there was the rigidity of tension in the man's stance: and his troubled feelings were finding only slight relief as he regularly struck the palm of his hand more forcefully than was usual with the silver handle of the cane. The pleasurable satisfaction bordering on glee he had experienced when Tomas Zalamero delivered the Gatling guns was long gone now; and Edge wondered briefly if Cutler was in part concerned by shame that he had indulged in such a high degree of delight at a time when he was preparing to avenge the brutality which the Apaches had visited upon his family. Maybe . . . but, maybe too, Jefferson Cutler was irked by his decision to wait it out at the fort until the Apaches came to him: when his forward plan had been to hunt down the Indians. And he could be especially embittered because he had not been allowed to reach the decision of his own free will: that it had been forced upon him by the contemptuous way in which the Indians had twice shown they were close by and able to strike at will.

Hell, there were a hundred and one vexing thoughts that could be gnawing at the mind of Jefferson Cutler. And maybe none were caused by the burden of command. He could simply be worrying whether revenge was going to be as sweet as he had hoped, especially since the price of the sugar had risen so steeply. Whatever the man's problems, they were no business of Edge. He had been paid his ten bucks yesterday and, so the rumour ran, each man's name was on an envelope on a desk in the commander's officer and in each envelope was a thick wad of bills that totalled two thousand and ten dollars. This, and the knowledge that he was in a well constructed fort in the company of a bunch of men who would kill with as much compunction as most would step on a bug, was sufficient to leave the half-breed satisfied with his lot. For he had put his life on the line for a great deal less money in tighter spots than this before: and on some of those occasions the smell of impending evil had been even more cloyingly strong in the air.

Madonna submitted to Phil Turner's insistent demands for the binoculars and quoted in response to Collins' comment on Cutler's change of plan: '"The best laid schemes o' mice an' men . . ."'

'What?' big Jack Maloney growled.

'Robert Burns,' the mean-eyed young man replied absently. 'A poet, from Scotland.'

'Hey, Madonna reads poetry!' Maloney yelled contemptuously.

'I read lots of everythin'!'

'Reckon that could be why you got that Mad Mike tag?' John Driver suggested, and laughed. 'Too much readin' can addle your brain as well as ruin your eyesight.'

'Least it ain't give me a friggin' squinty eye!' Madonna countered, his temper rising.

Driver was in the grip of a hotter rage than the younger men as he whirled into a fighting stance and started: 'Nobody talks about my——'

'Look, there's some guy over on the west ridge!' Lew Collins shouted.

His voice was loud enough to carry to all parts of the fort. And as the men on the walls strained to peer in the direction the black bearded man pointed, Breslin rocked upright out of his chair and Cutler took a first stride away from the porch.

'It's an Injun!' Turner reported as he focused the binoculars.

'Apache?' somebody asked.

'Just the one?' another man demanded to know.

Edge murmured as saw the mounted brave on the far side of the valley: 'It sure ain't Hiawatha. And I figure the others won't be long, feller.'

17

THE LONE Apache astride his pony was naked above his weapons belt and wore leggings below. His chest and face were daubed with warpaint and he wore a single feather held to the back of his head by a band. In his left hand he held a Winchester rifle. In his right, a pair of binoculars which he raised to his eyes a moment after he halted his mount on the skyline.

These details were reported to the rest of the now silent men by Phil Turner, who was allowed to keep the binoculars while everyone else scanned his distant surroundings for more Indians.

Then Cutler reached the top of the ladder at the far end of the walkway, closely followed by Breslin, who yelled:

'Make way there, friends! Turner, glasses for the major!'

Madonna growled: 'Winchester rifles and binoculars! Them Apaches sure are well supplied!'

'Stole the stuff, the thievin' sonsofbitches!' John Driver muttered vehemently.

'More likely did a deal with that Zalamero asshole!' the game-legged Drew Peppard added. 'The kind that are in the business of sellin' guns ain't never fussy who they do business with!'

The man Edge knew only as George rasped: 'And four good guys we could use now went down on account of that double dealin' bastard!'

A low murmuring of agreement with this sentiment was checked when Jefferson Cutler said evenly: 'Whatever kind of man Tomas Zalamero is, I am the kind who keeps his word . . .'

He was holding the binoculars up to his eyes with one hand while the other was fisted around the cane that he pressed to his side with his upper arm. When he started to defend his deal with the gun-running Mexican, his stance was as steady as his tone of voice. But then he saw something through the magnifying lenses that erupted choking bile into his throat and drained his body of much of what held it so erect.

'. . . Oh, dear God in heaven!' he gasped. And even as Breslin reached out a hand to support his swaying form, Cutler swallowed the burning acid and forced himself back up to his full, rigidly-held height.

The Apaches obviously knew much about the thirst for vengeance that Jefferson Cutler was so desperate to slake. The rich man had never made any secret of his intentions, and it had taken several weeks for his planning to reach fruition. So maybe the lone brave who was training the binoculars on *El Alcazar de San Juan* even knew what this particular White Eyes looked like. Or, Edge thought, more probably the Apache made an educated guess that it was Cutler who had been handed the other pair of binoculars so readily.

The brave had lowered his glasses and they hung down his painted chest on a neck cord. Then he had raised his rifle, one handed and sideways on above his head, and brandished it in a beckoning gesture. And three more mounted figures showed themselves on the skyline, which was when Cutler had come close to nausea and fainting.

'Major?' Breslin asked anxiously.

Cutler said in a rasping whisper as he wrenched the binoculars down from his eyes that had never looked so stonily lifeless: 'It's Lydia, Ben.'

The revelation was heard only by the men close to the northern end of the west wall. But the news that it was Cutler's wife out there on the top of the hill across the valley was hissed sibilantly along the line to the far end. This as Breslin accepted the binoculars from the major but checked the move to raise them to his eyes. Like everyone else on the walkway employed the wider angle vision of his

180

naked eyes to watch what was happening on the western ridge. Where one Apache seemed to be hewn from solid rock as he sat his pony, an arm still thrusting his rifle aloft. And two more slapped the rump of the pony that was between them. To set the animal galloping down the slope, trailing an elongated cloud of dust.

The rider on its back was not seen to be a woman until she had been carried close to the foot of the hillside. For until then the animal's burden might well have been loosely filled sacks fashioned into human shape: tied to its back in such a way that the sacks jerked and waved and flopped limply in response to every headlong stride, but were never in danger of being thrown to the ground.

Then the pony started to slow. Moved at a trot as it started to cross the flat bottom land of the valley. Walked a few yards and came to an uneasy halt. Scraped at the ground and tossed its head on the fringe of the former campsite littered with decomposed flesh.

Only now could it be seen that Lydia Cutler was not as flaccidly dead as it had appeared while the pony galloped down the slope. For when the animal beneath her came to a stop, she raised her chin up off her chest and gazed about her. Showed no reaction to what she saw.

'Sonofabitch, Major,' Breslin gasped. 'We gotta do——'

The woman was scantily clothed in buckskin breech-clouts and a waistcoat that exposed her legs from hips to feet and only partially covered her breasts. Her legs were skinny and her breasts were small. Her face was as lean as the rest of her, framed by hair that was probably much blonder when it was at its best. Now it was lank and matted and filthy. Also, her skin was ingrained with the dirt of many days, perhaps weeks. There was about the sparseness of her flesh a strong suggestion that it was due to recent starvation. In the way she had raised her head, looked about her, apparently seen nothing and then dropped her chin to her naked chest again, it seemed that many of her recent experiences had driven her into an unfeeling brand of insanity. Her ankles were tied to the stirrups, her wrists to the saddle horn and a length of rope encircled her chest and passed under each armpit to hold her upright against a three feet long piece of timber fixed to the back of the saddle.

A rifle shot interrupted what Breslin was saying. And all eyes that had started to switch their attention toward him and Cutler were abruptly drawn to peer again at the maltreated woman trapped to the back of the pony. Were in time to see the animal drop where it stood, a torrent of blood gushing from a wound where its left eye had been.

If Lydia Cutler uttered a cry of alarm or pain as she was forced to crash to the ground, one leg trapped beneath the carcass, it was masked by the barrage of gunfire that followed immediately in the wake of the shot that killed the pony. These shots exploded by Edge and a half dozen other men as they whirled into fast turns and aimed their rifles upwards. Ignored the dead horse and its captive rider. Also turned their backs on the long line of warpainted braves who had moved forward to skyline themselves as the isolated rifle shot served its second purpose as a signal.

And the brave on the ridge above the south east corner of the fort was not quick enough to beat the fast reflexes of the men who were momentarily unperturbed by the sight of so many of his Apache brothers. Was hit by most of the bullets exploded up at him as he rose and was half turned to take a first stride toward cover. And a moment later was spread-eagled, face down on the bare rock slope above the name of the fort picked out in the hillside: rivulets of crimson flowing out of his wounds to become the predominant colour on his painted back.

Then the preliminaries were over, and the death of their sharpshooter seemed to imbue the braves on the west ridge with a degree of ferocity that they perhaps otherwise would not have had. While, in much the same way, many of the hired guns on the west wall walkway were as affected by the sight of the human wreckage that was Lydia Cutler as was her husband. And responded immediately to the orders that were yelled at them. Swarmed down the ladders or spread out along the top of the wall with gun hammers cocked, but fire held.

There were more than fifty, perhaps as many as seventy warpainted braves spurring their ponies to a headlong gallop down the western flank of the San Juan Valley. And for long moments in the wake of the volley of shots that spilled the first human blood of the battle, just the ever-rising volume of the thudding unshod hooves broke the silence of the borderland at mid-morning outside the walls of the fort. While inside, the voices of men rang out, cursing, as they urged others and often themselves to greater effort. And on the top of the west wall the majority of white men half crouched in an almost silent line, rifles aimed.

Somebody spoke softly and rapidly the words of a prayer for deliverence.

Somebody else uttered a string of obscenities in the same low tones.

The gates were unfastened and Pierce Browning stood by one, George by the other. A quartet of men, Breslin and Cutler two of them, dragged one of the Gatling gun-mounted wagons across the square. And swung it around so that it was tail-on to the gates. As soon as it was in position, Cutler clambered up onto it, losing his cane in the process. And Breslin yelled an order at their two helpers, who whirled and raced for the stable. Next Breslin snarled a command that the gates be swung open.

Drew Peppard triggered a shot from the top of the west wall toward the area of the south east ridge where the Apache sniper lay in an inert sprawl.

'What the frig?' Jack Maloney groaned after glancing up in that direction.

'I thought I saw——' Peppard began to excuse himself in a whining tone.

'It's only good on a moonless night, feller,' Edge said. 'Or for one hot shot who figured surprise would give him time to get clear.'

'Asshole!' Harry Bean accused the shame-faced Peppard.

The Apaches had advanced to a midway point down the

slope, holding a steady line at high speed. The gates of the fort were open. Two men were hurrying out of the stable with a pair of horses, intent upon hitching them to the second wagon with a Gatling gun fixed on the back. Ed Walsh swung his apprehensive gaze from the empty northern stretch of the trail and was made suddenly more fearful as he found his eyes locked across a dozen feet with those of Edge. But it was neither the time nor the place to discuss the knifing of Dale Fish so that he could serve as a silent substitute for the actual Federal agent he had overheard talking with Sterling Schroder.

For the Apaches loosed an opening barrage. And the moment the puffs of muzzle smoke signalled the rattle of gunfire that would follow, the men on the wall squeezed their triggers.

Bullets pitted the wall, cracked over it or fell short. One glanced off the top of Harry Bean's Winchester and tunnelled into the bridge of his nose. Bean it was who had been uttering the obscenities and now he had time to call upon the Almighty before he died, sat down on his rump and toppled into the fort.

The fire from Cutler's men was more accurate. For they were standing braced on firm adobe instead of being astride jolting ponies. And after their reply to the Indians' volley, four braves had tumbled from their saddles, gouting blood and screaming their agony and fear against the whooping and hollering of the rest. Edge did not know if he could claim one of the hits. And he did not care. For the instant after he had triggered the first shot he was pumping the repeater action and raking the muzzle along the line of braves to locate a new random target.

He fired again. As did the line of men stretching away on his left. And the braves who were down off *he slope now.

Mike Madonna took a bullet in the shoulder and gasped. But only took a half pace backwards under the impact. Jacked a fresh round into the breech of his Winchester. A man who had a cot close to Edge in the barrack was hit in the throat and joined Bean at the base of the wall.

Some more Apaches toppled through the billowing dust kicked up by their racing ponies.

Browning and his partner raced away from the open gates to crouch at the wagon with the Gatling manned by Cutler and Breslin, one either side of the drawpole. Then both of them shoved. And the wagon rolled slowly through the gateway. Then, while Breslin began to shoot a rifle as soon as he had a field of fire, Cutler started to crank the Gatling: kneeling down behind it and sweeping it back and forth across a broad arc.

Drew Peppard had been hit by then, in the chest right of centre, and was sitting down on the top of the walkway trying to staunch the flow of blood from the wound. Harry Driver was bleeding from the side of the head but was still on his feet and loosing off a regular string of shots. Two more men were down at the base of the wall, one of them complaining that he was in bad shape.

More Apaches were down. The rest were turning their ponies, sheering away to left and right several yards short of the dry wash and trail. They fired when they were sideways on and then they turned in their saddles and exploded a hail of bullets behind them. But against the constant fusillade of rifle fire, the chatter of the Gatling gun was the dominant sound as its ten barrels sprayed out a deadly hail of bullets.

Then there was a sudden lull in the battle. Almost as if a time out had been called in the shooting. To allow the Apaches a chance to withdraw out of range and regroup. Which was not what had happened at all, of course. It was just that the braves abandoned their shooting for effect behind them as they galloped their ponies back up the hill. And the whites elected to take the opportunity to reload and so have full magazines in readiness for the next attack.

In the relative quiet, the men hitching horses to the second wagon with a Gatling on the back could be heard cursing the uncooperative animals and their own clumsiness. And then Cutler commanded:

'Shove this vehicle down the hill!'

185

Breslin yelled: 'But, Major . . .'

'Put your Goddamn backs into it!' Cutler snarled.

Pierce Browning and George looked from Breslin to Cutler, then at each other. And on the second order from the man who was paying them so highly they leaned hard against the wagon and took a half dozen short, half-running steps when the wheels began to turn. The wagon rolled away from the open gates at slow speed, under manpower. Then started down the sloping spur much faster, carried by its own momentum.

'Crazy sonofabitch!' Jack Maloney accused with a slow shake of his head.

'Guess you ain't never loved someone like he does,' Madonna rasped through teeth clenched against the hurt of his wound.

'Very friggin' poetic!' the big man said scornfully.

'Go to hell,' the younger one came back in the same pained tone.

'That's where Cutler and his buddy are bound pretty soon, I figure,' Maloney countered, less forcefully.

This as all the men on the wall found their attention drawn away from the Apaches for a few moments. To watch the wagon approach the foot of the slope, then make the flat. And begin to slow as it trundled across the main trail and on to the rough ground of the dry wash bank, then the creek bed itself. Both Cutler and Breslin had been clinging to the jolting wagon until then, probably as convinced as any of the watchers that it would crash and topple over: maybe crush them beneath its weight. But this was only one danger, averted after the wagon jerked to a halt. Some thirty yards from where Lydia Cutler lay trapped to the back of the pony, looking to be as dead and still as the sacrificed animal. Now the two men were vulnerable to a hail of bullets from the Apaches. Breslin as he crouched behind the Gatling, its insecure cover all that shielded him from the flying lead that would reply to his fire. And Cutler as he went at a stumbling run over totally open ground to reach his wife.

'He ain't even drawn his sidearm,' Phil Turner pointed

out unnecessarily as the Indians reined in their horses and wheeled them, closing up their line to fill in the gaps left by their casualties. Braves who were either dead or elected to play dead as their ponies galloped away from the stench of drifting gunsmoke, oozing blood and hovering death.

'If he does,' Lew Collins muttered, 'the poor bastard might just as well put it to his own head.'

The Apaches waited silently in their re-formed line on the slope, just outside of effective rifle range from the fort. Which meant they could have easily gunned down Cutler and Breslin at the dry wash. But no order was given by their chief. And it seemed to the watching whites that the Indians were again awaiting a signal.

Many men nervously eyed the ridge above the fort. But Ed Walsh peered hard along the north trail.

Jefferson Cutler reached his objective and pitched to the ground: as if from exhaustion instead of by his own volition. Close enough to his punished wife to embrace her and press her head to his face for stretched seconds.

The chief thrust his rifle high into the air again, and Edge could sense the elation that the Apaches were experiencing. Each brave fanatically prepared to die in the certain knowledge that the leader of the White Eyes was at their mercy. The half-breed was also aware of Breslin crouching more tensely behind the Gatling. Glimpsed Cutler working with anxious haste to unfasten the knots that made his wife a prisoner. Thought: *the stupid sonofabitch didn't even think to take a knife.* Then found himself drawn to look at Ed Walsh when every other man on the top of the wall, wounded and able-bodied, tensed himself to loose off a barrage of covering fire at the Apaches. And was in time to see an anguished look on the face of the bald headed man become a broad smile.

Then Walsh was conscious of being watched, and shifted his gaze to the face of Edge. Broadened his smile to one of heartfelt relief as he gestured with a nod for the impassive half-breed to look to the north.

Just as a distant bugle sounded.

The same call was heard by everyone else: Apaches and

whites alike. And it seemed like time stood still in the hot, bright morning as all eyes peered toward its source. Saw the front riders of a cavalry troop as they emerged from the shimmering heat haze at a headlong gallop, dust billowing behind them and company pennant flying above.

'Man, oh man, ain't that a pretty sight then?' Jack Maloney gasped.

One of the army deserters allowed: 'I said I never wanted to see a friggin' uniform again, but have I changed my friggin' mind!'

'We ain't hearin' things?' one of the men with the now hitched-up second Gatling gun wagon yelled.

The Apache chief gestured with his rifle and shrieked an order.

Edge squeezed off a shot, pumped the repeater action and the second bullet from his rifle was part of a fusillade that cracked out from the top of the wall.

Then Ben Breslin began to crank the Gatling. Which unleashed a short burst: before it jammed.

Jefferson Cutler called upon the strength of desperation to drag the limp form of his wife from under the dead weight of the pony. Then hurled her into the slight cover of the carcase and threw himself on top of her. Only now drew his revolver as a volley of rifle shots dug up divots from the dirt on all sides of him.

Breslin abandoned his frantic attempt to unjam the Gatling and drew his Colt as he made to leap down off the wagon. Was hit by several bullets and corkscrewed to the ground amid a spray of blood.

The second gun wagon raced across the square and out through the gateway. The driver did not slow the team on the slope and the man on the gun began to fire as soon as he could see his targets. And, like Breslin before him, this man may have dropped a number of braves as he raked the rapid firing gun back and forth. It was impossible to tell. For the line of men with repeaters also kept up a constant barrage as the attackers raced into range: seemingly intent upon mass suicide if that was what it would cost to kill Jefferson Cutler.

Then a new sound penetrated the pandemonium of the battle's noise. And it was startling enough to enforce a pause in the shooting from both sides. As all eyes peered to the south now. Where a second bugle blast signalled the presence of another column of uniformed men. Grey clad Mexican cavalry. Heading along the trail at a canter. Then spreading out into a galloping line of advance: as broad as that into which the United States troopers had moved.

The Apaches wrenched on their reins to demand high speed turns from their mounts. And viciously thudded in their heels to drive the ponies into faster gallops up the hill than when they had lunged downward. Their numbers had been reduced by perhaps a third by Cutler's highly paid army. Some of who now took careful aim and exploded shots toward any of the downed braves who showed signs of life. This as the US and Mexican cavalry troopers swung across the western side of the San Juan valley, in hot pursuit of the surviving Indians who raced in full retreat over the ridge.

Both bugles continued to sound the call to charge, counterpointing the thunder of pumping hooves. The sporadic shooting at Apaches who may just have been wounded was the only gunfire now.

Edge did not take a hand in this. Stood for a few moments with his rifle canted to his shoulder, looking impassively down at where Jefferson Cutler knelt beside his wife, holding her hand and talking to her. By some twist of fate both had survived the murderous barrage of lead that the Apaches had rained down at them.

The driver of the second gun wagon had not. Neither had Lew Collins nor Ed Walsh up on the wall. Down at the gateway, the freckle-faced Pierce Browning was sprawled out on his back, as deathly still as the rest. Their bodies or heads run with blood.

Jack Maloney was unscathed. So was Phil Turner. Some others whose names were unknown to the half-breed. Harry Driver's head wound was no longer bleeding. Drew Peppard was unconscious. Mike Madonna was unbuttoning his shirt to get a close look at the bullet wound in his right shoulder.

Gunfire sounded, muted by distance, from beyond the western flank of the valley. There was no more shooting from the wall of the fort, but the acrid taint of black powder smoke remained strong: like it was impregnated in the clothing of the men, or even their skin.

The half-breed leaned forward to spit over the wall to the outside of the fort. And glimpsed a lone horseman emerging from the heat shimmer out on the north trail. Then he went to the ladder and started down. At the foot of the wall, a man whose name he thought was Ted lay sprawled on his back, a massive stain of almost dried blood spread over his shirt from the waist to halfway up his chest.

'Hey, mister,' he called in a rasping whisper, reaching out with a weakened hand. 'I figure I'm in grave need . . .'

His hand dropped back to the ground and his eyes glazed with death: remained open.

Edge said: 'That's surely what you need.'

18

THE RUMOURS about the envelopes on the desk in the office of the fort commander were right. Edge found the one with his name on it, checked its contents and then went to the stable, where he saddled his gelding. He rode the horse across the brightly sunlit square at a slow walk, rolling a cigarette.

No one else had descended off the wall. A couple of men who had been down in the fort had gone up there: all of them watching for the re-appearance of the troopers, maybe. Or watching and waiting for Jefferson Cutler to make a move that might mean more money to be earned.

Some eyes glanced at him as the clop of the gelding's hooves resounded between the façades of the buildings that ran along three sides of the fort. Then he was through the gateway and a part of the scene beyond the confines of *El Alcazar de San Juan.*

Where dead Apaches were sprawled on the hillside, their ponies wandering aimlessly among them.

Where Breslin and the driver of the second wagon lay utterly still beside the two vehicles, the team in the traces of one of them waiting patiently for new commands.

Where Jefferson Cutler was on his feet beside the dead pony, encouraging his near-naked wife to rise up off her haunches: the man seemingly as oblivious to all else as the woman.

And where the tall skinny Sheriff Sterling Schroder sat astride his halted horse at the point where the spur to the fort gateway angled away from the main trail.

The lawman nodded as Edge drew near.

The half-breed said after lighting his cigarette: 'Walsh is dead.'

Schroder grimaced, then shrugged and answered: 'He knew the risks that went with the job.'

'Nobody else knew. It was an Apache bullet that put him down.' Edge reined in his gelding.

The Crooked Creek sheriff spread a more deeply-lined grimace over his face and spat out of the side of his mouth before he growled bitterly: 'None of this needed to happen, Edge. That mule-headed Cutler just couldn't wait. He knew it was only a matter of time before Washington and Mexico City agreed to joint action against the Apaches in this area.'

They both looked toward Jefferson and Lydia Cutler as the woman came unsteadily to her feet, and the half-breed said as he made to heel his horse forward: 'I guess he figured he was the kind of man who could afford to do what a man has to do.'

The woman showed a first sign of being intelligently aware of her surroundings. Held out her arms toward her husband. And he made to embrace her, calling out her name. But then she sprang back from him. And he vented an anguished moan of despair. For she had snatched the revolver from his holster. Now thumbed back the hammer. Turned the gun. Bent her head down to it, her mouth gaping. Closed her lips around the muzzle. Steadied her gun hand by grasping its wrist with the other. Squeezed the trigger. Crumpled her emaciated body to the ground in front of her horrified husband while the blood and gore and bone that had exploded from the top of her head was still splashing through the air.

And Edge said as he started away from the shocked lawman: 'And it figures that after what she's suffered, it could never be enough just to bite the bullet.'